MYAH CATHERINE

In Her Eyes

kindle | direct publish

First published by Kindle Direct Publishing 2020

Copyright © 2020 by Myah Catherine

All rights reserved. No part of this publication may be reproduced, stored or transmitted in any form or by any means, electronic, mechanical, photocopying, recording, scanning, or otherwise without written permission from the publisher. It is illegal to copy this book, post it to a website, or distribute it by any other means without permission.

This novel is entirely a work of fiction. The names, characters and incidents portrayed in it are the work of the author's imagination. Any resemblance to actual persons, living or dead, events or localities is entirely coincidental.

Myah Catherine asserts the moral right to be identified as the author of this work.

Myah Catherine has no responsibility for the persistence or accuracy of URLs for external or third-party Internet Websites referred to in this publication and does not guarantee that any content on such Websites is, or will remain, accurate or appropriate.

Designations used by companies to distinguish their products are often claimed as trademarks. All brand names and product names used in this book and on its cover are trade names, service marks, trademarks and registered trademarks of their respective owners. The publishers and the book are not associated with any product or vendor mentioned in this book. None of the companies referenced within the book have endorsed the book.

First edition

This book was professionally typeset on Reedsy.
Find out more at reedsy.com

To my husband Calven, your encouragement and enthusiasm keeps me moving forward.
To my daughter Jinorah, I hope this teaches you to chase your dreams.
To my Lord and saviour, thank you.

Contents

1	The Chocolate Baby Girl	1
2	I am the Freak	8
3	Changing Faces	15
4	Monsters Hidden Beneath Bad British Accents	22
5	The New Girl Blues	29
6	Trapped in the Classroom	36
7	Perfection	43
8	Seriously	49
9	I'm a Horny Confused Idiot	56
10	No… Ok Maybe	62
11	The Devil on My Shoulder	70
12	God Let Me Hate Him a Little	77
13	Six Hours	83
14	I'm So Lost	90
15	What a New Year	98
16	Days without Darien	106
17	Can I Kiss You Again?	116
18	Overwhelmed	130
19	Opening Old Wounds	141
20	The Truth Hurts	153
21	Pain is So Damn Painful	164
22	Starting Again	170
23	Eia Au, Eia 'Oe ~ Here I am, Here you are	175
About the Author		182
Also by Myah Catherine		183

One

The Chocolate Baby Girl

My father always wanted a girl. He wanted a precious little girl that he could love and cherish as his own forever. The baby girl that he could watch grow up and protect from all harm and wrong doings. She would run to him when she had a booboo and would climb on his back so she could reach the stars. The girl that would get her heartbroken and cry in her daddy's arms until he made it better and then fall in love all over again. She would dress up like a vision for her prom and stand proudly on the stage for her graduation. The little girl he would one day walk down the aisle and give away to the man of her dreams.

Married to his high school sweetheart, he knew that his child would be the most beautiful creature to grace this earth because his wife was breathtakingly beautiful and he was a handsome man himself so his child would be all of that and then some. That was what he wanted, what he got though, was three little boys. Triplets to be exact. Adam, Adrian and Alec Wilson. "Strapping adolescent boys" his father would say. And although he was more than happy to have his boys, deep down he still wanted a girl.

Five years later and God had heard his pleas and blessed him with a baby girl. A baby that made him cry every night with tears of joy. A baby to which he named Arabella, meaning "Answered prayer" or "Beautiful", what a perfect name for a perfect daughter. But perfect, she was not.

As the weeks went by the lucky couple realized that little Arabella wasn't as beautiful as her name made her out to be. No. Arabella was different, not special, just different. Different because little Arabella had Heterochromia of the eye... two unique eye colours. And no, they were not the beautiful brown like her older brothers and her parents... no, she couldn't be even a little normal. Instead, she had one crystal blue eye and hazel eye.

And I know what you're thinking, "Oh, okay, that's not that bad! I mean, I'm sure she got that eye colour from her grandparents or something. Right? RIGHT?"

WRONG!

Because this girl just couldn't catch a break, could she? No. Arabella was a rare case that even the doctors couldn't explain.

"What do you mean?" You ask?

Well Heterochromia of the eye means a person is lacking melanin and in most cases it is common for the case to be partial or sectoral heterochromia in which part of the iris is a unique colour from its other. For those who do not know, eye colour in the iris is determined mainly by the concentration and distribution of melanin. In layman's terms that means that since little Arabella's family has brown eyes that means that she would have one brown eye and one hazel eye as she was being created in the womb. Simple as that.

NOT!

Can it get any weirder? Oh yes, it can as there are no recorded family members with either blue eyes or hazel eyes for fifty years. Let alone the fact that they are so deep and bright which is almost impossible. So baby Arabella was no angel and was no precious chocolate skinned girl. No, Arabella was a freak. A complete and utter abomination.

I am that freak.

I am that girl that has to go to family gatherings to have everyone question why does she look so funny? I am that girl that had to run into daddy's arms crying all the time because my cousins thought I beamed here by aliens and made fun of me by saying "E.T. GO HOME!". I am the one that tainted by people's mean words and accusatory looks so much, that I can't find any beauty in myself anymore.

"Wow, that's so sad!" You would say while shaking your head. "Maybe you should go to counselling or talk to someone about your pain." And I would laugh because that wouldn't be the first time I had heard that suggestion.

Or maybe you might say "Hey I know you may have had it rough but there's always a rainbow after the rain," or something like that right? You're just too sweet… and too naïve. Naive because you think I would catch a break in my life, right?

I mean "It couldn't have been terrible you're entire life." Wrong again.

My childhood was a nightmare. Children are cruel evil insignificant creatures that like to pick and pick and pick until you are a destroyed scab left lying somewhere broken, battered and torn apart. They love to tease and mock and joke around with things they do not understand because it's easier that way. They love to point out the obvious flaws in a person's stature to prove that they are so much better than you. They like to chew you up and spit you out because you taste, smell and look like fear. And fear tastes good to them. Fear keeps them going. Fear makes them thrive.

"But you've got to be exaggerating!" You would say. "They're just kids! They can't be that bad!"

You would think because who knows, maybe when you were younger you were that kid. That manipulative child that used the big words you heard your mommy and daddy say and threw them at a defenseless baby girl who didn't know any better.

Maybe you were once the child that was smart enough to know that using physical abuse would get you into trouble, but mental abuse? Verbal abuse? Oh yes. That defenseless girl wouldn't be able to withstand those words. Those simple but concise words that still stick with you to this day.

I grew up in a suburban neighbourhood in New York City. We weren't rich, but we had a suitable amount of money… still do. This neighbourhood comprised two types of kids, blonde hair and blue eyes or brown hair and brown eyes. Sure there was the occasional ginger or the rare black person with perfect caramel skin and beautiful brown eyes, but it was rare for a reason. And somehow, no matter how different those two rarities were, they always accepted them faster than me.

So imagine a girl with black hair and two unique eye colours that were too bright to be hidden as a kid. Technically, I was half of each category of child, yet it wasn't good enough... are you beginning to get the picture? See, in that suburban hell everyone was perfect. They walked the same; they ate the same food; they knew all the same shows and jokes. Hell, they even sounded the same, and I didn't. I couldn't fit in no matter how hard I tried. No matter how many times I tried to straighten my wild curly hair, or even cut it off. No matter how many contacts I tried. They hated me because I was too different for their tastes. And they made sure I knew that every day.

"But come on! Kids don't know what they're doing or saying half the time!" And maybe you're right, but that doesn't help the fact that once those words are out, they're out.

Freak.

Monster.

Ugly.

Gross.

Weirdo.

Loser.

Mutant.

Bride of Frankenstein.

The Wicked Witch of the Ugly.

Yes, that last one was original. But those were just a few of the words I had heard daily. They seem so simple, don't they? They seem just like childish words, easy to brush off and grow out of. Because "Sticks and stones may break my bones, but words will never hurt me," right?

Wrong.

Positively wrong.

Just wrong.

Words hurt more than physical pain. Because physical pain will eventually go away. But words? Words stay planted in your mind. Words stab at your heart and your psyche and they bury deep within your subconscious to bite at you when you feel at your best. Words remind you you're not as great as you may think. And words... they only grow.

They have harsher sounds and more malicious meanings. They have more letters and uglier appearances.

They get louder.

And Louder.

AND LOUDER.

They scream at you even if you're right beside them. They take up their axes made of callous and offensive letters like "abnormality" and "anomaly" and "grotesque" and "monstrosity" and they hack at your self-confidence.

They chop

and chop

and chop

you down until you are nothing but fractured little pieces of yourself. That's how powerful words are. And that is my life.

"Wow kid... you've got issues." And I laugh at your blunt honesty because it's true. It's all too true.

I have a loving family that sees past my deformity and loves me for the weirdo I am. They love me for my laugh, which when I laugh too hard I snort, my ears that I can wiggle without touching. They love me for my artistic expression through the same thing that was used to beat me down. Words. For my fantastical stories and heartfelt poems. They love me for my full, coiled, black hair and brown skin. They love my snide comments and famous eye rolls. They love me for my... well, for my everything.

I've always appreciated the fact that they love me not because they have to but because they know me well enough to want to. And yes they are the family to remind me I am exactly what they wanted for a daughter because I am healthy, I am beautiful inside and out and I am a blessing from God. They see me as their daughter and not a monster and for that I am forever grateful. Without their love, there would have been a void within me that could never be filled.

A darkness that lives in my heart and mind that feeds me the nasty words that I've grown so used to hearing. A darkness that a part of me believes has never seen light before. A darkness that is so cold and so vile that every time I venture towards it, it snaps at me with vicious words, snarling and cursing at me for being me. For being such a freak. For being as my daddy says, "What God has made me".

But naïve little me believed that God could change me. I mean if this Almighty guy could raise the dead, make the blind see, the deaf hear and the lame speak then surely he could change my eye colour. SURELY! But no, nothing and my faith had shattered. How could someone so all powerful ignore my pleas? I just didn't want the bullying any more. I didn't want the pain or abuse. I didn't want to cry all the time.

But for now… I realize that even though he didn't answer my prayer; it wasn't bad. Because as I grew older I realized that if he had changed my eye colour than what? I would still deal with teasing, even more so than before. I would have still have mocking and people would really believe I was a witch and a monster. I would have been taking in for more testing and examinations and my life would have been a living hell. My life wouldn't have been my own any more than it would have been the world's. Can you imagine the T.V. shows that would want me on just to see the difference? The miraculous wonders that would have been my eyes?

"All right, all right kid quit preaching at me." And I apologize if things may have gotten a little intense just then for you, but it was your choice to read this so you just have to suck it up and continue.

"But why not just wear contacts? Everyone does it nowadays?" You ask while sighing at the simplicity of my situation.

Trust me, I tried that too! But they BURN my eyes. Burning so bad that I can't keep it in for more than a few seconds. What a shame, huh? I've tried prescription, I've tried over the counter and I've tried special order and none of them stick. It's like God's way of saying "Stop trying to change what you are."

It's such a mystery how the Almighty works up there. What he's thinking, what he's doing, why he made us the way he did. I mean, I still don't believe he's all that great. But I know he's there. Because it was his choice to give me three strong older brothers.

Brothers who are so similar and yet very different. Brothers that adore their little sister and cherish her like the outstanding little sister they see her as. Brothers that fought for me and defended me as much as they could even though they were five years older than me.

"Wait… doesn't them being older than you mean they could scare off the kids easier?" Yes, that is a good thought. Too bad it didn't apply to me.

See, when you have an older sibling they're like your guardian and fighter all in one. If something bad happens, then they have your back. The only problem is when they're five years older than you that would mean they aren't in the same school as you. That means they aren't even remotely close to you. So when you're getting bullied in middle school, they are flirting with girls in high school. When you're getting bullied in high school, they are flirting with girls in a college usually out of state. You see my point?

Regardless, they were ferocious for my protection. They would drive, fly or even take the train back to me if they thought I was in any kind of serious trouble. Girls, boys, men and women no matter their age or gender, all three of my brothers would go toe to toe for me. And because of that, I still have a little of faith in the Almighty. He didn't change me, but he blessed me with three angels that I couldn't be happier to have by my side.

"Where are you going with all this?" You must wonder by now.

By now your tears have probably already dried and you've grown tired of the sad brief story of Arabella Wilson. The wannabe chocolate baby girl that lives a life of shame for something she had no control over. Well, I will tell you this is only the beginning.

You see this isn't some kind of sob story in which I want your pity or something because believe me I've gotten enough of it from teachers and counselors (You see! I went to a counselor! Or three…) No, this story isn't about the fact that I've had to move five times in the past four years across the country, no less. This story isn't really about me, honestly. This story is about a boy.

A boy who bothered me endlessly and threw himself into my life. A boy who never took no for an answer. A boy who turned my life upside down and then turned it upright again.

A boy who changed everything.

Two

I am the Freak

Arabella Wilson

"Can you believe she's even allowed to be in this class with us?" *No I can't believe I'm in a class filled with annoying airheads that focus more on lip injections than they do on homework.*

"I heard she transferred to six schools because no one wanted to accept her." *Actually, I had to transfer to five schools because the bullying grew worse and worse at each one, not that you would care to know.*

"Well, she will never get a man looking like that, trust me." *Well I don't want a man so don't worry. Besides, if looking like you is how you get a man then I'm glad I'm different.*

"At least there's an upside to her being here... her brothers are so hot! Like literally lick off their abs delicious! I saw them drop her off this morning and oh my gosh, I almost fainted! They're triplets, can you believe that? And they're all so sexy!"

"I wonder what happened to her then."

"Not even she can get such a delicious gene."

I have to bite my tongue so I don't comment on that one. These girls… I mean, are they even allowed to be called girls with the way they look? No, let's go with aliens, these aliens are the epitome of the bimbo/cheerleader stereotype. Blonde hair, blue eyes, bee stabbed lips and too much makeup.

Actually, they kind of remind me of home… well, my first home in New York. At least their boobs are real and their butts are flat so they aren't too fake… Doesn't help their faces though. What did they call it back in the day, ratted up hair? That's what their hair looks like! A rat's nest!

"Can you see her lips? Can you say botched?" *Yes I can say botched, hell I watch the show, but unlike you my lips are 100% real thank you very much. A lush gift from my grandmother.*

"All right class, settle down." The teacher at the door says balancing a coffee, a book and a briefcase. He's a very good looking man with dark brown hair and even darker eyes. A chiseled jaw and full lips let alone the muscles bulging beneath his dress shirt. He doesn't even look like a typical teacher; he's too hot to be a teacher!

Placing everything down carefully, he glances around the classroom before his eyes settle on me. The smile that graces his lips makes my stomach churn and no not in the "Oh my gosh he is the most gorgeous teacher ever" way. More in the "Oh crap, he will call me up to introduce myself" way, which is something I do not want to do.

"Well, it looks like we have an extra student today. Do you mind standing up and telling us your name?"

My face heats at his annoying question and I stay glued to my seat. It's always the first day that's the worse.

"Come on, don't be shy. I'm sure we all want to meet you." I hear groans throughout the class.

He uses his hands to make the "stand up" motion and I sigh. Here we go. Standing up quickly, I allow my afro to drop into my eyes (thank God I have a good enough regiment that is this long).

"My name is Arabella Wilson." And just like that, I sit back down just as quickly and clench my fists.

"I guess it's good I have great hearing. Nice to meet you, Arabella Wilson, and welcome to Writer's Craft. Here you are free to express yourself through any form of writing that you deem fit. It's all about-"

"Creative expression." The class answers for him. Some roll their eyes while most, meaning the aliens, all sigh out in pleasure at the sight of him.

"I'm Mr. Remington but I'm cool with you calling me Vince or Vincent. I am a hard marker but a fun teacher. And now that the introductions are done, let's get started. You arrived at the perfect time Arabella we will write short stories about anything you want and tomorrow we will exchange them with a partner and both will add to the story what they deem appropriate, staying within the context." Murmurs of excitement buzz around, but I'm already starting to feel nauseous.

"It can be no less than one thousand words and has to follow a theme of struggle, freedom or perseverance. So now that you all know your instructions... get to work. You have the entire period."

Laptops and tablets are taken out simultaneously just as sheets of paper are being ripped and passed to neighbours. I never ask to borrow or use anything from anyone. If I can do things on my own, I will. Taking out my favourite notebook and the black and gold fountain pen my father gave me for my birthday, I get to work.

Writing has always come easy to me. Maybe it's because I never wanted to speak to people knowing the hurtful words that would come out of their mouth. Or maybe it's because my dad says my mind is an endless movie reel and the only way to get those fantastical images out is to write it on paper. Personally, I love to write because it relaxes me. It helps me to escape from reality just for a little while and be normal. Even though I know I'm not normal.

"She's such a freak! Who uses fountain pens anymore? Like hello twenty-first century!" The alien beside me giggles to her friend. Both of them laugh like hyenas, ugly laughs for ugly personalities.

"Yeah, I know. Like it doesn't even look expensive. Where did she get that from the dumpster?" Her alien friend responds by flicking back her poorly dyed yellow hair.

"Uh duh! She lives in a dumpster, she got it from there!" The alien hyenas cackle some more before Vince looks up and narrows his eyes.

They just bat their eyelashes and look down at their laptops, still giggling to themselves. How revolting. I plug in my earphones to my phone and play some calming music.

Yiruma is critical to calm my nerves. No one can get to me when he plays. The way his fingers dance across those white and black keys allows me the same ability to write fluently with my pen. Spring Time is my favourite song so far, such power, such peace… two things I may never have.

Decidedly I start my short story on the theme of struggle because I know all about it. I write about the depths of hurt this character goes through and the anger that bottles up within them. I open up the world of pain to this paper and write things that even scare me. The struggle, the heartache this character goes through almost makes me want to cry.

"Arabella!" Looking up I notice the class is almost empty and I jump up in surprise ripping my headphones out of the socket and destroying my serenity for the rest of the day.

"I'm sorry sir is class over?" Vince chuckles at my question and gestures to the empty room.

"You are very perceptive, Arabella. You should get going." I nod my head quickly and gather all of my stuff, silently mourning the loss of my peace. Walking past the smiling teacher, I race out of the room and scan my timetable for my next class.

This college is bigger than it showed on the website. George Washington College… such a boring yet patriotic name. I almost didn't apply this year because of lack of enthusiasm, but my parents pushed me and here I am. The campus thankfully is close to home as well, so it's not as bad as I thought and taking a bunch of useless classes to fill the year isn't that bad either.

Glancing back down to my timetable, I try to decipher where the hell to go in comparison with the useless map they gave me. Too bad I didn't see the giant in front of me as I trip into him, my books and papers flying everywhere and phone shattering on the ground. This is how you make a first impression for sure. I'll forever be the falling girl. What an outstanding nickname.

"Blimey! Are you all right beautiful?" If my face could get any hotter, it would melt by now. The giant with the sinful voice reaches down and helps me gather my things, but I'm quicker and snatch everything away from him. Standing up, I feel a little woozy causing me to sway a little and it seems the giant finds that funny.

"Hey love, don't get dodgy with me. I ain't going to hurt ya." His hand goes to my arm and I flinch away. Why can't he just leave? What do you say to a British giant that won't get the hint? Oh yes.

"Sod off!" I turn in the opposite direction and march all the way to the lab or maybe it's the athletics centre. I have no freaking clue where I am, but at least I'm away from him.

The rest of my day is sorrowful. Without my headphones I can't listen to music and if I can't listen to music, then I can't block out all the words that the alien hyenas use against me. It doesn't help either that my screen is so shattered that when I touched it I cut my finger. The stupid thing. So, so far this day has gone to hell.

"And did you know that?–"

"Did you know that the girl that you can't stop talking about is right beside you and can hear every word you're saying? Let alone the fact that you keep making stuff up to make the drama seem that much more interesting, which it isn't. Do you have nothing better to do with your life than to bother me?"

The girls look at each other, whose names I have learned are Lydia and Jessica, and narrow their eyes at me.

"I'm sorry was I talking to you?" *Why did I even say anything?*

"No, but you were talking about me."

"Jessica I don't know if I'm getting this right but do you remember me talking to this freak?" Her friend shakes her head so fast she looks like one of those bobble head dolls.

"That's what I thought. How about you take you trashy self and turn back to your work? No one here likes you or even cares about you." I roll my eyes and look at this annoying thing I have to tolerate for the rest of this semester.

"Trust me, there's nothing I want more than to ignore every stupid word that comes out of your mouth–"

"Oh my God, what is wrong with her eyes?" I freeze and lose every nasty word I would use against her. Why couldn't I have stayed quiet? I could have gone this entire year with no one seeing my deformity and now, out of everyone at this school, the girls with the loudest mouths just had to discover it. Just freaking great.

"She looks like such a... a... a freak! What a freak!" They cackle to themselves some more and whisper among themselves.

They're probably coming up with more evil words to say about me and even more creative names than freak. The lecture hall gets louder with jokes and laughter at Lydia's stupid comment. I can hear people taking out their phones to text each other and probably get pictures of me when I pass by them.

When class is out it seems everyone knows that I'm the falling girl or that I'm the freak with two unique eye colours. Apparently I'm all over Twitter. I walk into the commons area to get some lunch and I swear to you and the Almighty above that the entire place goes silent upon my entry. No word of a lie, it is dead quiet. I walk into line to get some food and keep my head down as people whisper and snicker all around me.

Keep calm Arabella. Remember your breathing. In and out. In and out. In and out.

I listen to the words of my last counselor from my high school in Texas and breathe slowly.

Their words mean nothing. Their words mean nothing. Their words mean nothing. Don't let them get to you, Arabella.

She was such a nice counselor, accent and all. She was one of the few that cared about my wellbeing and knew that there was a problem even before it presented itself. Ms. Debbie Brown, a beautiful brunette with bright green eyes, a button nose and thick lips that she admitted to getting fillers for. If it wasn't for her, I would still be in Texas, getting physically abused more than mentally. All for something that was an accident...

"Look at her. She's so weird. Who wears an afro anymore? Is this the seventies?"

"Trust me, she won't be here for long. Lydia, told Jessica, who told Alex, who told Maria, who told Steven, who told Kyle who was making out with me she's transferred to eight schools in the past two years." *Wow! Word gets around fast! Too bad it isn't true.*

Grabbing a slice of pizza, I hurry to pay for my food and leave the commons.

Not knowing where else to go, I head to the library and eat alone. I guess this is how this year will be. Thankfully, it's no different from before.
  Lonely.

Three

Changing Faces

Darien Petros

What is the point of college? I mean, seriously? I've been to six schools in the past three years, yes that's two schools per year, and there's nothing different. Even taking a year off before starting this hell hole and I still don't see any actual reason for being here.

They created college to further a student's quest for knowledge and prepare them for the working world… at least that's what my father tells me. But to me college does not differ from high school other than there are more girls, more classes and more places to have sex. What a big change. Half the time I don't even know why I applied to college. It's not like I have much of an idea of what I want to do with myself.

So instead I have made the best of this pointless year. That's the daunting task I have to take onto myself. Make each place memorable no matter the consequences.

If that must mean one year I am the wicked boy with poor grades and a poor attitude then so be it. If then that poor attitude gets me expelled from that school then you pull out the good boy card so your dad doesn't send you to military school.

And once that righteous boy act doesn't allow you to get laid, you act like the jock at the next school. It's easy since you excel in almost everything you do, anyway. But then rival schools love to fight causing you to get expelled again for handing a guy's ass to him.

So now you're the smart kid, outshine everyone else and excel more than you expect for yourself but that adds a load of pressure onto you you're not in the mood to handle.

Instead of moving to an unfamiliar state, you try out accents. Australian is a little harder than you'd like so once you move to your newest school you go for British and boy does it work. Only a month in the school year and you've been with three girls. Yes, this British one has to stay.

"Hey Darien, if you're not busy tonight-"

"I'll call you and let you know, love." The red heads are always the crazy ones. They like to do anything, try anything... say anything to please you. And please me they do. Such fun girls.

"How is it you're only here a month and all the girls want you? Technically, you're a freshman here!" My newest comrade Taylor asks me as he ogles the surrounding girls. I shrug my shoulders and smirk.

Girls are simple to manipulate. That's how, but I dare not say that out loud, of course. You see, girls are dramatic while guys are simple. Girls are mentally and verbally aroused while guys get physically aroused. Girls like guys who are fit and ripped while guys will take anything. Girls like actions that make a statement or declaration of love, guys don't give a crap.

So you use those things against them. You use words that are so beautiful and dirty to get them interested. You make sure you're in good physical condition all the time and flaunt that to those who are watching. You buy the girls flowers and cheap pretty things that make them feel special. You manipulate them until they feel like they are the most important person in the world... and then sex is a smile away. Simple.

"I'd say I'm lucky but we both know better than that don't we eh mates?" The girls all giggle at my joke and a brunette sidles up to me. Tugging on my collar, she pulls me down to her height and licks my ear lobe.

"Whenever you want to be with a genuine girl here's my number." A white piece of paper slides into my front pocket before she grips my hardening member. These girls always want to be with the top dog. They want to be the best and sleep with the most popular. They like being the wildest or the sluttiest or the most passionate. It's humbling to know that I will always be on top.

I glance down at my watch and see it's time for class.

"Sorry ladies but I'm not one for being tardy." The girls sigh and whine as the crowd disperses. Some girls stay behind to walk me to class, some leave me lingering looks before rushing away… all of them love me. Though the feeling isn't mutual. Sex is sex. I don't want or need love. It's a pointless emotion that does nothing more than cause pain.

"Man, I heard we have a new math teacher, and she is hot a hell!" Taylor says to Matt another person to join us.

"Yeah, I heard she has a body like Kim Kardashian."

"The question is lads, is she as nasty as Miss Kardashian?" I ask coyly. The guys all hit my arms in appreciation to the vivid images now plaguing all of our minds. Entering said math class, I am not disappointed with the rumors. The woman before me is curvaceous and thick in all the right areas and when she turns around, I already know I will have to find a girl to have a quickie with so this hard-on can leave me soon.

I've always enjoyed having smaller classes compared to the lecture halls because it gives you a better view to those around you. And the view this teacher is giving me right now is perfect.

"Morning class. My name is Bonita Lopez and I will be your calculus teacher. So if everyone could find their seats and get out your work tools then we can begin." Some guys hoot and holler when she bends down to get something from her bag, but I don't. I may be a dirty guy, but at least I know how to respect women, especially when they're my authority figures.

"I will do a roll call just so I can get to know you all better. Be warned I'm great with names and faces so try anything stupid and I will know who it was." She starts the attendance and I settle into my seat. It will be awhile before she reaches my name, anyway.

"Hey." I look over to Taylor on my right and he points to his phone. I take mine out and read his message.

In Her Eyes

Taylor: Would you do it?

It's obvious what he's asking me, so I give him an honest answer.

Darien: If she weren't my teacher... absolutely.

I watch from my peripheral as Taylor grins and puts his phone away.

"Darien Petros?" My signature smile dances its way onto my face as I take in my Latina teacher. Gorgeous.

"Here Bonita." She smiles back and continues the list. You know, I'm sure it wouldn't be hard for me to charm her out of her pants. In fact, I'm sure it would be easy, but I'm not in the mood for switching schools again. If I've learned anything in life, it's that when you do stupid things, they always come back to haunt you.

"All right class it's great to meet you. Before we begin are there questions?" Almost every guy's hand raises and Bonita rolls her eyes.

"Any question that isn't sexual?" The hands go down slowly and I laugh. Instead, I raise my hand in curiosity.

"Yes..." she looks down at the attendance and then back up to me, "Darien."

"I'm just wondering what happened to Ian? He was our teacher for a bit and then he just vanished... not that I'm complaining." Lopez nods her head, obviously relived that my question is general.

"Ian was covering for my maternity leave that extended longer than I expected. But I will be your permanent teacher for the semester. Any more questions?" No one says a word so Bonita gets to work.

***

"Can you believe someone so sexy could be so evil?" Taylor asks rubbing at his forehead.

"Yeah man she killed my boner so quick." Taylor laughs at Matt and they both turn to me.

"Well, it is calculus what did you expect mate?" Both guys shrug and head across the campus to their next class. Since I have a free period, I lounge around for a bit before I go to get some proper breakfast, maybe even some sex at a girl's house. Anything is possible.

"Darien, wait up!" I turn to see Lydia Biggs rushing down the hall to me. The girl is such a contradiction to her last name. There is nothing big about

18

her other than her lips, which I've been told aren't real. Her long pin straight blonde hair and her crystal blue eyes maybe a turn on for most guys here but not for me. I've got a thing for girl's with darker hair. She was a mistake I never intend to make again.

Terrible things happen when you have too many shots of tequila. Things like being coercedsed into having a threesome with those two girls. A threesome that was so rushed and forced that I had to fake an orgasm so I could leave faster.

Her bimbo friend Jessica Thompson rushes behind her with her corn looking hair and her horrible sloppy lips. God, that was a night I really want to forget.

"Darien, I've heard you have a free period right now. Maybe you want to do something?" Her hand snakes up my chest and I shiver. Sadly Lydia takes it as excitement went its revulsion.

"I'm sorry ladies I can't right now but I'll give you a bell yeah?" Pulling away from her, I back up and practically run down the hall and straight into someone. Her startled gasp is adorable and when her books fly in the air I'm reminded of a nerd in a movie suddenly. You know, the one that always hides away and wants no contact with people because they're super weird.

"Blimey! Are you all right beautiful?" Through the curtain of her hair I can see her cheeks tinting red and I smile to myself. Every girl loves this accent. It's like sex with a voice.

Reaching down, I try to help her gather everything but she's pretty determined to keep me away, to where she rushes to grab everything and jumps up. The poor thing rocks on her heels and I can't help laughing. She's adorable and so small. She's not even at my shoulder, standing up straight. It's like she's a tiny kid!

"Hey love don't get dodgy with me I ain't going to hurt ya." I tell her trying to reach out and steady her. Maybe we could have a quickie. Younger girls are always so much more desperate to please a man. Her body flinches away from me and I notice she is getting frustrated. It looks like she's almost talking to herself before she finally speaks.

"Sod off!" And she flies down the hallway and out of sight. Her accent was strong I wonder if she's actually British. Shrugging, I continue heading down the hallway as everyone goes to their next class. I pass the girl's washroom and hear some weird murmurs, so I knock on the door to make sure whoever is in there is ok. When no one responds I walk away, but then a hand reaches out and pulls me into the bathroom.

There are two girls in here and one of them has her top off while the other, the one who grabbed me, is panting.

"Ooh its Darien!" The girl who's topless says.

"Yes… and who are you lovelies and what exactly are ya doing?" The topless girl blushes and pulls at her straps.

"Experimenting." I raise an eyebrow at that and walk forward. The girl who grabbed me locks the door and I smirk.

"Experimenting, eh? You mind if I watch?" They both giggle.

"My name's Erica and this is Sarah." The topless girl says closing the space between us.

"And if I will experiment I figure I will need two subjects… don't you?" I groan when she grips my bulge and pull her in for a kiss. This is an excellent way to waste time.

***

"Are you serious or are you just trying to make me jealous?" I look over to Matt and roll my eyes.

"Why would I care to make ya jealous lad? Whateva 'appened, 'appened and it was bloody good." Taylor laughs out and Matt frowns.

"Fine prove it. Where are these imaginary girls?" I point to our left where Erica and Sarah are sitting and wave them over. What we did in that bathroom was both invigorating and so sexually stimulating I'm getting aroused just thinking about it.

"Hi Darien." I point to the hickey on her collarbone and give Matt an enormous smile.

"Enough proof?" He nods and the table laughs.

I'm a little surprised that the girls aren't embarrassed about what we did. I'm also surprised no one knocked on the bathroom door once during the duration of our experimenting.

I continue to laugh until I realize that the commons area has quieted down. Looking around, I see the girl from earlier walk in and people whisper about her. I barely pay attention to what they're saying because I don't care, but I continue to watch her as she keeps her head down the entire time she's here. Her full curly hair looks so soft and bouncy from here. I wonder what it would be like to touch it. I kind of like the way it looks on her.

All too quickly she gets her food, and she's gone and the noise gets louder than before. And while everyone was talking mindlessly before she walked in, now it seems she is the main and only topic of discussion. Who is she?

Four

Monsters Hidden Beneath Bad British Accents

Arabella

"So, what exactly happened Ari?" I sigh into my dinner and pull my hair up into a bun. I don't hide my deformity from my family. They love me regardless, the saps.

"I was working on an assignment and didn't realize class finished. When the teacher called me, I freaked and ripped the headphones." I tell my dad as sweetly as possible. I know regardless he will buy everything back, but I have to at least give him an excellent reason first.

"And what about your phone?" My mom asks, setting a bowl of coleslaw.

"I bumped into some giant that couldn't watch where he was going, and it fell to the ground. I have more than enough money saved up to buy back both." Dad grunts and looks to me disapprovingly.

"You'll do no such thing, Arabella. We can go buy you a new one right after dinner." Dad says kindly.

Mom rolls her eyes and places the bread on the table. She knows dad would do anything for me because he loves me so much. He's admitted to everyone at a family gathering that I was his favourite.

Ever since my brothers came back from college, mom has resorted back to making more food than necessary. Tonight, we're having jerk chicken with rice, me and Alec's favourite dish by mom. But the amount she makes is like a crime. I mean, we could feed a third world country with all of this food.

"Who was the giant Belle? Do you want us to come over to that campus and handle him?" I hit Adam on the shoulder and laugh.

Adam is the oldest by fifteen minutes, and he's always been the most protective of me. He's also my favourite but I would never tell my other brothers that. I guess it's because he relates to me the best.

When he was younger, he loved to write poems and he was talented. He would go to competitions and win awards. So, we can relate so easily for writing. And he's also the most caring of all three of them. Whenever my parents would work late, he would tuck me in and read to me or we'd watch a movie together until I fell asleep. Adam was always the one that would come into my room in the middle of the night when I was crying because of the monsters under my bed and he'd scare them away. He's always watching out for me.

"It's no big deal Adam really." I say picking at my salad.

"And what about those catty girls? Are more girls bothering you?" You see, this happens when you tell your brothers about the bullying at school. You have one moment of weakness and they never let you forget it.

"They aren't as bad in college Alec." Alec is the youngest out of the three and also the fighter. He's beaten up guys who bullied me and got girls to beat up the girls who bullied me. He's like the protector. He's even beaten up guys that would pick on my brothers. He just loves to fight. It's why I figured he'd want to be a UFC fighter or something. But he said he doesn't want to ruin his pretty face.

"I don't want you to lie because you don't want us to intervene Ella. Seriously we would only talk to your associate Dean." And that's Adrian the smarty pants.

He's obviously the second born. Adrian is so smart he was able to skip a grade! He graduated before my brothers with such ease that he spent a year just travelling the states and finding his passion. When he came back he immediately knew what he wanted to do and decided to wait until my brother's graduated as well before he went off to college.

We connect on the intellectual level. I excel in math and so does he, so we have this game where we would take random numbers on and create equations from it. It's a lot of fun and super challenging… ok it's fun to us.

"You guys, I'm fine, really. I can handle these bimbos with no sweat." They all chant "Super Nova" and bang their fists against the table and I shake my head.

Super Nova is a nickname the kids at my school in Georgia called me after I blew up on some guy that said the only reason, I looked so ugly was because my parents were deformed freaks. I can take the insults no problem, but no one talks about my family. I had to switch schools.

"All right enough. It's time to eat. Arabella, can you say grace?" I nod my head and watch as everyone bows their heads and closes their eyes.

I'm not as spiritual as the rest of my family. Years and years of praying to God to change your eye colour can do that to you. I'm not bitter or anything, just a little jaded… but that doesn't mean I don't believe in him. Sure I do!

I've read the Bible I know of his works and wonders and I know he exists. It's just I don't care to pray to him all that much or talk to him often either. But I still go to church! I like church. The singing and the colours and the events are always fun… Besides I know one day I'll be accepted for who I am and people will cease the teasing and the non-sense and leave me be… sounds believable right? Right.

"Dear Lord, we thank you for this food and we ask you to bless it and bless the hands that made it. We love you and appreciate all you have done. Amen." The family joins in with their rehearsed *amen* and we all dig in.

"You know one day I'd like to find a girl that can eat like Ari." I look to Adam with my mouth still full of chicken and smile.

"Well your sister is one of a kind, isn't she?" All four of us roll our eyes at mom's statement.

"Yeah, she's special mom but I'm serious! Most girls are always so cautious and picky with what they eat! When are chicks going to just enjoy food and eat whatever they want?"

"Maybe when you stop calling them chicks." I reply with my mouth full of garlic bread. Adrian laughs at it and Adam shrugs.

"Do you guys remember when we lived in Georgia for a year?" Adrian asks. Well, this is random.

"Yeah, the girls were so hot!" Alec says throwing his head back.

"Yeah, but they weren't as hot as the girls from Virginia! They were sexy." Adam responds.

"Those Texan girls would have been perfect if it weren't for their annoying accents." Adrian adds.

"Hey, I liked the accents." I throw in. Alec nods in agreement.

"Let's just all agree that girls are beautiful and should not be objectified merely their appearance. Right Jacob?" My dad looks at all of us and then our mom before he nods his head.

Smart move, dad, smart move.

***

"Did you want the same phone as last time?"

What started as a father-daughter trip turned into a family outing, not that I mind? If people snicker and comment on my deformity, I have my brothers to protect me. They're all big guys, so every time they glare, the jokes stop.

"I'd prefer a phone that won't break every time I drop it."

"So that's a no to Apple then." Adam says laughing. I laugh with him.

"Definitely no Apple."

"I've 'eard Samsung is quite good." My heart stammers at the sound of that voice. But it can't be him. It just can't! My brother, dad and I all turn around to that sinful voice. Oh, damn it… it's him.

"Ello lovely. Wonderful to see you again." I hate his voice… absolutely hate it.

"Ari? Who's this?" Adam asks, already moving to stand partially in front of me.

"The giant." I mutter under my breath. My coils fall forward, and I try to ignore his piercing stare.

"Who?"

"Darien Petros at your service, mate." He thrusts his hand out for both my father and Adam to shake and they do so slowly.

"And may I finally have the pleasure of knowing your name beautiful?" Why does he keep calling me that? Why must he keep lying to me? In front of my family, no less! Does he have no decency?

"Her name isn't beautiful so you can cut it out." Adam says aggressively. Darien shows amusement in his eyes as he examines the two of us.

"I would say I meant no offense but there was nothing offensive about what I said. She's a pretty little thing she is. I just 'aven't gotten her name yet mate."

"Arabella." I hiss. Looking up to him, I see something happen with his eyes. It's like his pupils dilate for a split second before he smiles even wider.

"What a perfect name." I hear him murmur and it's almost as if his accent fades a little before, he continues talking.

"It's a pleasure to meet ya officially. And I apologize about this mornin'. I was runnin' from someone." I scoff at that and turn away. Sure, he was. More like trying to embarrass me! Does he even know the ridicule I had to endure by the alien hyenas because they believe I threw myself at him? How disgusting!

"We can find the phone somewhere else, dad. Let's go." Adam is right behind me as I leave the shop and dad isn't too far back. I turn back to see Darien staring at me, still with those intense eyes. They make him look older and much more serious than he lets on to be. Almost as if it is the window into who this Darien character really is...

Gosh, Arabella, stop over analyzing and just run away.

"You sure you don't want me to deal with him Ari?" I shake my head and keep walking. The farther I am from him and that damn voice, the better I will feel.

"Arabella I think that's the only cellphone shop in this mall. It is pretty small." Dad says slowing down. As I come to a halt, I realize he's right. Crap.

"Oh... yeah right. Well let's find mom and the boys and maybe I can get a better opinion on what phone to get." Dad looks at me quizzically before agreeing.

"That way we can all leave at the same time." He leads the way ahead and I let my hair fall forward. There aren't many students from school here, but I know a few of the faces so far. Adam comes to my side and throws an arm over my shoulder.

"If they say anything, I will handle it." He already knows. My brother isn't blind or stupid.

"Thanks." A slight smile graces my lips and he smiles, back. Even though I am more than capable of fighting my own battles, it's good to know I have three brothers to keep me happy and safe.

We find the rest of my family at Starbucks.

"Shouldn't you have a phone by now Ella?" Adrian says smirking. I roll my eyes and flick his chest.

"Nah, she was busy ogling some British guy." Adam says casually. I growl at him and punch his arm as hard as I can.

"I was not ogling him! I don't even know him!" Alec walks over to us laughing with some girl. He's always with a girl in or out of the house.

"Well, he knows you. And he likes you." Adam chimes and my face heats again. How can a guy I literally just met like me? And I thought the Brit was being cruel.

"Don't say something like that. Ever. It's a lie and its stupid so let's get this damn phone already. I just want to go home." I say walking away. I already know they will apologize, but it doesn't make this any less hurtful.

"What's wrong with Arabella?" I hear my mom ask from behind.

I continue to keep my head down and sulk like the deformed freak I am. Why did I have to go to college? It's not like it's doing me any good. Maybe I can run away and hide in Disneyland at least that way I can wear one of their costumes and no one will see my... well at least I'd be in Disneyland.

"Ari slow down! We're sorry! Come on Ar- Wait, look out!" I turn to their voice and hit a wall. A very warm, solid wall. A wall that can vibrate.

"It's not that I don't fancy running into you love but every time it seems you're in shambles yeah?" His arms wrap around me to steady my fumbling feet and I can't help leaning into him.

He smells like Old Spice... it's a very mature scent that has this alluring appeal to it I almost want to–NO! He's just like the rest of them. He'll try to get close to me and then his true colours will show and he will be a monster. They're all monsters hidden beneath pretty faces, expensive clothes and British accents.

"Can you let me go?" I ask quietly. He's making me feel uncomfortable and fuzzy. He's nothing but trouble.

"What was that love?" I'm about to look up at him when I hear footsteps approaching.

"Let her go." His arms flex around me as I hear Alec's voice. Obviously, he dropped the desperate girl hanging off his arm. I can feel Darien's heartbeat pick up as he quietly assesses my brothers and then he chuckles.

"I thought one of you was bad enough. You've got three of them beautiful? Must be hard to chat up mates when they're up your arse, yeah?" A part of me oddly wants to laugh at his joke and tell him he's right… even though I rarely ever talk to guys, but the better part of me, the part that knows he's just trying to get under my skin pulls out of his grasp.

"Can we please go?" I ask, falling behind Adam unintentionally. His arm wraps around me and Alec steps up.

"Listen kid stay away from our baby sister or we'll kick your-"

"I said let's go!" My voice comes out sharp and annoyed and Alec reluctantly steps back mumbling under his breath. We all turn to walk away, but then I stop and look at Darien.

"And next time Darien don't touch me… I'd rather fall." His face looks confused as I turn back to my brothers. Adam keeps me on his side as we leave Darien behind. This time I don't look back.

Five

The New Girl Blues

Darien

 I've always wondered what it would be like to get rejected by a girl. I figured she would be of some model statuesque with legs for days and eyes that say, "Do me Now and Do me Hard." She would be older obviously and the rejection would sting but I would get over it, eventually. Never in my life could I imagine this.

 Watching that beautifully frustrating dark skinned girl walk away with her three older brothers guarding her like watch dogs bothers me more than I would ever admit out loud. I mean come on! It's not as if I was earnestly pursuing her! I was barely even flirting with the girl and she still walks away from me as if I'm the scum of the Earth. How offensive.

 I feel a vibration in my pocket and force myself to tear my eyes away from Arabella's retreating back. A very nice looking back at that.

 Matt: Dude party tonight my place! Let's get wasted!

 A party would be an excellent distraction from such an indifferent day so far… But throwing a party in the middle of the week is both reckless and stupid. I'm not wasting my time.

 Darien: Can't busy

 Matt: Aww man come on! That dirty red head said she wants to-

In Her Eyes

"Darien how many times must I tell you to stop texting on the job?" Locking my phone, I put on my best smile for my manager Sarah, a boorish brunette with a desperate need for a makeover and a man.

"Aww love don't look at me like that yeah? I was just texting me mum ya see?" Her cheeks tint pink and she places, a hair behind her ear slowly.

"Oh, I'm sorry I didn't know. Just be quick about it, you still have an hour left in your shift." She turns to walk away before she stops and stares at me again.

"What are you doing over here, anyway? The store isn't portable." My eyes glance towards the now vacant hallway that Arabella was once walking.

"It's nothing." I don't even try to fake the accent.

***

I end up deciding to go to Matt's party because I have nothing better to do.

By the time I get there, the party is in full swing. There's music blaring so loud I can hear it inside my car and drunks are littering the lawn. Most of them are puking or sleeping and each one is in a position so funny they look a little like garden gnomes. Shutting off my car, I head inside and go straight to the kitchen.

"Darien! Man, I thought you said you weren't coming?"

"Finished work early." Matt smiles wide and hands me a drink.

"Let's get drunk!" I smile with him but disregard the drink. I am not waking up tomorrow morning with a killer hangover. No thanks.

I watch as the crowd jumps and dances to Martin Garrix's "Animals" and I bob my head to the beat. I've never been much of a dancer before. I prefer standing on the outskirts and watching people… or doing other things.

If I were to be honest with myself, then I'd admit that I hate parties. I hate them. All they do is cause destruction.I have first- hand experience of what a party can do to a person… how it can damage a person and scar for life. If I've learned anything within the past twenty years of my life, it's that terrible things always happen… always.

Memories flash in my mind, and my mood continues to darken. And this party isn't helping either. I watch as these desperate… no, these pathetic guys are hitting on girls who don't know their true intentions. The liquor causes these poor girls to be blind to the disgusting and perverted looks these boys are giving them. Looks that are promising dirty things, in dirty places.

Everyone here is either drinking or smoking or dry humping each other like animals. Sucking each other's faces off and slobbering all over them. A complete disregard for decency.

"Hey Darien." I can't even smile when I see Erica and Sarah again.

"Ladies." They both giggle and move closer to me.

"So earlier today... it was so hot." Erica says boldly.

"Yeah so hot." Sarah echoes.

"And we were wondering if you're willing to do it again?" I sigh and shake my head.

"Not tonight, love." They frown and walk away, blending into the dancing crowd.

Throwing my head back, I close my eyes and a curtain of ebony hair fills my vision; Wild black hair with tight curls that fall just at her shoulders and frame a round cute face. A shapely figure with gorgeous rich brown skin, smooth to the touch. A scent of jasmine wafts through my senses and I try with all my might to cling to that heavenly smell. A voice so soft and alluring that can draw in all who hear.

Arabella.

God, her name is so damn attractive. And her attitude, her mannerisms, her resistance. It's all such a pull. I can still see her walking away from me with such confidence and ferocity. I've never encountered someone who didn't want me... someone who could *see* me. Now that I've met her... I don't know what to do.

***

"What's up with you lately, man? It's like you're sad or something." Taylor asks me as we drive to the nearest burger joint for lunch. I can't stand cafeteria food, it's almost as bad as McDonald's.

"I'm not sure what ya mean?"

I know exactly what he means, and it's been damn well bugging me too! I haven't seen, heard or bumped into Arabella all week. I mean, what the hell? I haven't gotten my retribution for her ditching me the way she did.

"Yeah right. Ever since last week you've been quiet, well quieter than usual that is. I mean, I heard you only slept with like one girl all week. One girl! Are you sick or something?" *Yeah sick in the head.*

"Your concern for me is touching you wanker but I ain't about to spill out me feelings to ya. This ain't Oprah." Matt laughs in the back seat and Taylor rolls his eyes.

"I'm not trying to be your doctor or anything like that you've just got me worried is all man. Sure, we may not have known each other that long but you're still my bud."

"Thanks."

I pull into the drive thru and we order our lunches. Driving up to the window we happen upon a very busty woman with bright blue eyes. She eyes me and then my friends in the car before she smiles slowly and seductively. Licking her lips, she opens the window and leans forward for all to see her ample cleavage. She's young and it's obvious to tell by the unnecessary amount of makeup she's wearing. The girl bites her lip and bats her eyes at me. She wants my attention…

"That'll be twenty-one fifty nine."

I think about flirting with her, maybe even getting her to go on break early and take a ride on me, but the way she's looking at me… I just don't want it. Not now, at least. I give her the money and drive through without another word.

"Dude did you see her rack! Why didn't you say anything?" I roll my eyes and grab the food.

"She looks like a daft cow. It'd be a boring shag and I ain't up for it." Matt and Taylor exchange looks before they take their burgers as I just continue driving.

It's not as though I haven't had sex because of Arabella. There is no way some random girl will stop me from doing that; I'm just not in the mood for it.

"Man, I'm not feeling class. You guys want to skip?" Matt asks as we pull into the school parking lot. I turn off the car and give him a hard look.

"Why the bloody hell would you say that now you wanker? We're already here." He laughs uneasily and scratches his head.

" Yeah, I know but I was eating when I thought about it so I couldn't say anything yet." Taylor laughs at his stupidity and I shake my head.

"I can't skip me pops would blow. Besides, we're almost done mate. Let's get it over with, yeah?" Taylor's already out of the car and I'm just opening the door when Matt grumbles a yes.

That feisty brunette from a few days ago eyes me down before she saunters over to me. Can't these girls cut me some slack? I haven't even eaten my lunch yet.

"Hey there Darien." Her hand slides up my chest and I raise an eyebrow at her bluntness.

"Hi... I'm sorry, what was your name, love?" She giggles and reaches up to my ear, flicking her tongue into my earlobe. I'd be disgusted if I weren't putting on act.

"Hailey."

"Well then Hailey, how can I be of service?" I can feel her breath on my skin as she walks in front of me to wrap her arms around my neck.

"My place is a five-minute walk from here and no one is home right now." A grimace makes its way onto my face, but I fight it back and give her a weak smile. She's been watching and flirting with me for a week now. She seems... desperate, but hey who needs lunch I guess. I try to smile wider as I lean down to her ear.

"Lead the way." Her arms unwrap from me and she smirks at the surrounding girls before taking my hand and leading me to her house. Taylor and Matt laugh as they high five each other and nod when I walk past them.

The residences are lined up in rows all along the school perimeter, so when we leave I notice she isn't lying when she tells me her house isn't far. I can still partially hear the chatter of people from her doorstep right now. Walking in I keep an ear out for anyone who may be in the house but it's quiet.

"We can do it anywhere you want." She says behind me as she closes the door. Her house is modest with natural lighting and the powerful smell of cats. The furniture is new and covered in plastic and everything seems to be organized according to its use. Meaning there's no way in hell I will bang this girl in the living room without her roommates knowing and possibly freaking. That's too much drama for me.

Bedroom it is.

"Let's go upstairs, yeah?" Hailey pulls my hand forward and up the flight of stairs to the pinkest room I have ever seen. I mean seriously everything is pink, her pillows, bedsheets, walls, curtains, even her damn rug.

I suppress a shiver and watch as she slowly strips for me. Her top gets thrown to her dresser and her leggings follow suit. I watch as she unclasps her bra and drops it to the floor dramatically before she slides off her thong and stands before me bare and excited.

"Do you what you want, Darien. I can take it all." In most cases I would be more than excited to screw around with this girl, but for some strange reason I'm still not in the mood. I walk towards her to break the grave news but she turns around and lets her hair down. It's frizzy enough that it could pass and a flash of Arabella hits my mind as I grow hard.

I know it's probably immature of me to imagine Arabella here instead of this girl, but I can't help it. She won't leave my damn mind.

Continuing my walk towards her, I slowly assess her body. She's got full breasts that would definitely take two hands to hold, a long torso that accentuates her hour-glass figure and small but nice ass. I doubt this is Arabella looks naked, skin colour alone, but that's the point of imagination.

"Do you like what you see?"

Again, Arabella flashes in my mind. Her attitude fierce, her lips full, her hair free and bouncing.

"Abso-bloody-lutely." I cup her globe in my hands, squeeze and listen as she hisses. She's a sensitive girl. Oh, that will make this that much better. I gently push her down on her bed and thank God I restocked the condoms in my wallet.

***

When I get back to school my class is already thirty minutes in. Just great. I could skip, but I decide against it. Putting on my best smile, I walk in the lecture hall while the teacher is talking. Everyone looks over to me and I continue smiling even though I just want to go home. I can't stand being late, it draws too much unwanted attention to me.

"Oh, Mr. Petros, how nice of you to join us. Take a seat."

"Sir. Sorry I'm late." He tsks as I smile even harder and climb the steps to sit in the back.

I don't know many of the people in this class so I usually keep to myself. I could be social, but I don't care to when it's the end of the day. Instead I lean back and drift off as my teacher talks about the depth of psychology and all of its importance.

I don't even know why I took this class. I care little for psychology or helping people with it. I don't even want a career in psychology... hell, I don't even know what I want to do in life.

I took an easy Communications certificate in hopes I'd find something that I was good at but nothing minds. Once upon a time there was something that I excelled in, something that I could even in my sleep I was so good... but... I can't do that anymore... I shouldn't even be thinking about it.

Why am I thinking about it?

Hey Darien!" My eyes focus in front of me and I see Taylor sitting on a desk nearby.

"What is it?" He looks around the class and raises his eyebrows. Everyone is gone. Real smooth Darien you probably looked like an idiot just spacing out all this time.

"Dude the day's done. Let's get out of here." I nod and follow him to my car, thankfully leaving those memories behind.

Six

Trapped in the Classroom

Arabella

Avoiding Darien was easier than I thought since he's always draped with desperate lust-filled girls anyway. Literally, I've been able to walk right past him and he still wouldn't even see me… but that's a good thing. No one should have the burden of seeing me anyway.

From listening to the unrelenting mouth of the alien hyenas I've learned that he is a man whore… ok, that's not the way they put it. No, instead they said that he "is a sex God with the body of Adonis and the drive of a horse". Not surprising in the least bit. Just as I suspected, he's just like the rest of them. What a waste of time.

Playing keep away with Darien the British Man Whore and ignoring the alien hyenas had become a routine so easy that the first month of college flew by. Sure I have to deal with those plastic little spastics every week in two of my five classes, but I have a savior. Vincent Remington.

Vincent has become my favourite teacher and just about the only person I can talk to about anything whether or not I want to.

A few days after the run in with Darien, he found me sulking in his classroom eating lunch.

Flashback

"Hey there, Arabella. Mind if I ask why you're alone?" I look up to see Vincent hanging in the doorway of his classroom I am occupying. I knew I should have stuck to the library.

"I prefer to be alone." His eyebrows quirk at my answer and he takes a hesitant step forward.

"Well am I allowed to stay in here as well? I can leave if it will bother you." I'm touched that he even cares to ask. I mean, this is his class room. I heard that he fought with the Dean to keep this room specifically as his own because of the prestigious reputation and relationships he has with his students. There was a whole thing about it and in the end... he won.

"I can't keep you from your own class, sir. Be my guest." He smiles and leaves the door partially closed behind him.

"Do you mind if I play music?" I nod and continue to nibble on my sandwich.

My eyes glance down at my story that's been critiqued by a student in class. They said it "would be an outstanding story if only it wasn't written by such a freak". The girl was one of Lydia's friends and they both cackled when she handed the paper to me. I erased the words before Vincent could see them, but that doesn't mean I can't still see the etching... Doesn't help that I can still feel it too.

The soft tones of "Indigo" play and I feel my heart skip a beat. My head shoots up and I watch as Vincent continues to unpack his own lunch while he throws his feet up on the table. My mouth drops open at the shock and I can barely get the words out of my mouth.

"Vin-Mr. Remington sir... you listen to Yiruma?" His eyes fall onto me lazily and he smiles again.

"Yeah, I'm surprised you even know who he is!"

"I could say the same to you sir." He turns up the song some more and closes his eyes for a few seconds.

"Some girls in my class a few years ago kept playing this song that's related to the Twilight books. They called it the unofficial Bella's lullaby. They played it so much it's forever cemented in my mind, so I looked the artist up. Turns out he's damn amazing. I've been hooked ever since."

My smile becomes apparent and I unconsciously push back my hair. His mouth quirks and his eyes narrow. He's seen it. Stupid move, Ari. Stupid move.

"Your eyes..." I let my hair fall forward again and look away.

"Yeah, I know."

"They're amazing. Arabella, they're so cool! I've always found people with one eye colour to be boring. You know the typical blue, brown and hazel, nothing different, nothing to set them apart... and I guess that includes me too. But you, my God, you have such a uniqueness in those eyes."

A blush burns my cheeks at his compliment. No one's ever been that nice to me about my deformity before. Maybe things will change when I graduate college. Maybe not.

"Thank you... I'm often teased about my defor- my eyes." Vincent rolls his eyes and laughs lightly.

"Kids are mean and bored, and you don't deserve to be on the receiving end. But even though it may hurt, have you ever thought of why they bully you?" My head snaps up at that question and I can't help rolling my eyes.

"Yes, isn't it obvious? They think I'm a freak. They fear me because I'm not normal. They are afraid of the unknown." I say the last part quoting Ms. Brown.

"That may be true. But I know for a fact that beneath all of that teasing those girls and maybe even guys can't help but notice just how special you are. There's a beauty within you that they can't ignore and though there are better ways at addressing it, these kids still do." I remain silent at his comment and he takes that as the end of our conversation.

What he's saying can't be true. I've grown up with too much hurt to believe otherwise.

End of Flashback*

After that I decided that Vincent needs more of Yiruma and brought him his newest CD as a thank you for letting me eat in his classroom.

I guess that was when it started. He may not be my friend, but he is someone I've learned I can depend on. The only one in this boring school that I can rely on and I prefer it that way.

No one can mock me when I'm around him because they don't want to cause trouble and since he's such a likeable guy and an avid fan of Yiruma, we have more than enough to talk about. He even helps me with my writing techniques. And yes, I will admit sometimes I have low points and I stare at his ridiculously good-looking body. I can't help it if he's too hot to be teaching!

I usually spend my break in his classroom unless I have to study to which the library then becomes my sanctuary, but I'd rather hang with him. He's good company.

***

Today is Halloween… yes, Halloween on a Friday is always the best. And not surprising that the girls, the alien hyenas, celebrated by dressing up like Britney Spears in her "Hit Me Baby One More Time" music video; short skirts, white button up shirts tied at the stomach and pigtails… how classy.

"Good morning everyone and Happy Halloween. I figured since it's such a special day we could do something a little more fun than usual. So here's my proposal…"

As Vincent gives instructions, I space out. I've heard rumors about the pranks on freshman at this college. You'd think people would mature and become adults as they venture into post-secondary school, but you're sadly mistaken. They're much more immature than before.

Apparently sometimes people get hosed down with silly string or they wake up and their hair is dyed a new colour. Usually these pranks are more closely compared to the hazing athletes undergo, which is a little disconcerting. One guy was tied down to a chair and had whipped cream covering his family jewels. When he finally broke free he had to run around the campus to find his clothes.

My mind wanders and I think back to life in Texas again. Next to New York, that's the only place I spent more than a year or two in. Middle school wasn't as bad as high school. The kids were mean, yes, but they didn't care much either.

It was mainly the girls that bothered me because they believed I was trying to look pretty and take their boyfriends. Which is stupid, I know because I was purposely trying to look ugly? I spent two years wearing my brothers' oversized clothing in high school so they would leave me alone. And it worked. It worked perfectly until the tenth grade.

See, I was very good at being invisible. I could get through class every day without being called on and without getting picked on. I grew out my hair so I could get front bangs that would cover my eyes well enough and nobody really noticed me. Everything was perfect.

But one day in gym class when I had no clothes to change into, I had to go to the lost and found to find something to wear. Now no one goes to the lost and found because it's in this tiny room with nasty smelling clothes. It's just a no-no to go to, so I don't know I did.

As I wondered if there would be any decent clothes to find, what I found was two boys playing with each other's body parts very sexually. I didn't know what else to do other than squeak, which I now know was a stupid thing to do. When they turned and saw me, they freaked out and ran at me. One started rushing to pull up his pants and one of them still had his pants down and he jumped on me knocking us both to the ground. The door shut closed, and it trapped me.

So now I had a half-naked guy, whose girlfriend was one of my favourite bullies, rubbing his stuff on my leg and putting a hand over my mouth to keep quiet. Was I scared? Oh yes, but not that he would rape me, obviously because I could tell I wasn't his type. I was more afraid of getting caught and people thinking about something other than what was happening. I squirmed and fought under him for him to let me go and he fought to keep me down and quiet.

One of the many things that popped into my head at the time was,
"Why didn't he just pull up his pants and run?"

But he never answered the question. The other boy had run away and left and I could oddly enough hear this boy, his name was Marcus, I could hear him moaning out.

Can you believe it! He was attacking and restraining me and yet he was getting turned on by it! I guess he wasn't as gay as I thought. I remember him moaning and groaning that it felt good and him positioning himself as he rubbed on me.

Did I feel violated at the time? No, I was just worried about the bullying getting worse if anyone saw us.

Do I feel violated now? No, not really because I was wearing my brother's baggy jeans that were thick enough that I couldn't really feel anything. Thankfully, he didn't think to grope my breasts or anything like that.

Was it nasty as hell? Oh yes.

All I wanted was to get up and run and forget any of that had happened and I would have too. When he realized I had stopped fighting one minute of gyrating ago, he asked me,

"If I let you go will you say anything?"

I shook my head no and his stare hardened.

"Do you swear?" I nodded quickly, and he finally got off of me.

Just as he was pulling up his pants, and I stood up his girlfriend found us. That day I got the snot beaten out of me. You don't mess with girls from Texas, that's for sure. Especially when that girl thinks you're trying to steal her bi-sexual boyfriend.

After that, for two years I was bullied constantly because she thought I was trying to give her boyfriend oral sex. I tried to tell her he was secretly in the closet, but she said I was a liar and a snake. I even went to Marcus and told him to tell her the truth, but he ignored me. I had to take advanced courses so I could graduate a semester earlier than the rest of my class.

Such a pity for me I had to move again, I really loved Texas.

Focusing back on the present, I look down at my blank piece of paper and then towards Vincent. It's obvious that I wasn't paying attention, but he doesn't comment on it. The class ends and I gather up my things to head to my Shakespeare class. Oddly enough, today the alien hyenas didn't bother me once. Like at all. Not a word or a snicker. Not even a glance in my direction. Maybe they've finally grown up.

Saying goodbye to Vincent I head out the classroom and weave through the hordes of people to get to my next class. This teacher, Mr. David, is super strict with attendance and tardiness so I pick up the pace. As I'm about to reach the building to his class, I get this ominous feeling that people are following me.

Looking behind, I notice the alien hyenas are directly behind me in a straight line. A bunch of other people are walking with them, most of them guys that are jocks. They're trying to act inconspicuous, but they are way too obvious.

I try to walk as fast as I can to class, but one jock grabs me from behind and carries me into an empty lecture hall. My first thought is that he will rape me but when he runs out laughing and locks the door I clue in to what's happening.

I can hear their laughter from outside and I bang on the door for them to let me out. Someone big blocks my sight. He looks like one of the football players with a buzz cut and a huge build. I continue to bang on the door for five minutes straight before I give up. Checking my phone, I see class starts in five minutes and I try not to cry.

I will get in so much trouble with Mr. David! He will probably give me a zero!

Slumping against the door opposite the bulky jock, I close my eyes and imagine that I'm anywhere but here. And it's peaceful for all of five seconds. The door opens up and I fall backwards. I prepare myself for the impact but I am safe in someone's arms. Probably a teacher. Opening my eyes, I look up and groan.

"You all right, love?"

You've got to be kidding me.

Seven

Perfection

Darien

"Don't look so upset, love. I didn't ask to be here neither."

We've been in here for thirty minutes now and she still won't calm down. It's like she can't stand to be in here with me. Which is insulting since I am such friendly company.

I watch as she twists her hair around her finger anxiously, probably a nervous habit. Her thick hair seems to cover her face, like she's trying to shelter herself from something or someone. Maybe she doesn't want me to remember that she's the girl that kept bumping into me. How cute. She's nervous!

"I don't have time for this. I need to get to class!" She says sounding both exasperated and a little hot.

Her pacing allows me a nice very of her round backside. It's cute and shapely like her and looks very sexy in those leggings. I've always loved the recent trend of leggings. While with some girls it just further emphasizes the fact that they have no shape, with Arabella it shapes it so perfectly that I'm getting aroused.

She bends over a desk to pick up some of her papers that fell with her pacing and I wonder if she's purposely trying to turn me on. I wonder if she

In Her Eyes

has a boyfriend… probably not with the way her brothers were sheltering her.

"Well yelling at me won't do ya good Arabella." It's the first time I've said her name out loud, let alone to her face. Her reaction makes me swell with pride. Even though her face is away from me, I can see she is flustered when I say her name like that. Ladies just can't resist the accent.

She continues to pace in front of me watching the clock for five more minutes and I watch eagerly as her breasts heave up and down with every breath. They're a lot bigger than I thought they would be and rounder. They'd probably feel soft and fit in my hand perfectly. I like breasts that I can hold with one hand, that way I can hold both at once. Twice the arousal.

After another few minutes she slows her pacing and acknowledges me again.

"I'm sorry. I need to calm down and make the best of this… whatever that may be." It barely comes out as a whisper and yet I hear it crystal clear.

She stops pacing and her hair falls forward again covering almost every visible aspect of her face something I never noticed before. What is she hiding? Does she even know that she's doing it?

"How about you sit down, and we get to know each other yea? We got time." I motion her to sit next to me and she sits across. No big deal. I don't mind the extra space. I gesture for her to begin, but she barely even looks at me.

"That's all right, I'll begin. So, I'm Darien–"

"I know that already."

"Yes right. Right then. Uh, I'm taking the Communications certificate program… for what reason I don't know."

"I'm in Creative Writing." I wonder just how creative she is…

"Cool. That's cool. I just moved here from Nevada."

"As in Las Vegas?"

"Yup." Her head bobs and I blow out a breath. She is not making this easy.

"How long have you been living in California?"

"I'm new here too."

"Oh really? Where did you move here from?" She plays with something on her desk before she speaks again.

"Texas."

"Oh? You don't really have the accent, I imagined. Were you born there?"

"No."

"So where were you born?" She shrugs.

"Where were you born?" She asks completely redirecting the question.

"Haw- Uh, I mean England?" I blurt catching myself. I don't know why, but I can't keep my head straight when I'm with her. Arabella laughs lightly and shakes her head.

"Whatever you say." I smile at her, even though she can't see it, grateful that she didn't further question my mishap. How about I redirect this conversation?

"Ok... um do you like this college?"

"No, do you?" *Good question.*

"Not really."

"Who would have guessed?" She says sarcastically. Either she is bipolar, or she just enjoys putting on a show.

"What's that supposed to mean?" She still won't look at me and it's starting to bother me.

"It means... nothing." We both sit in silence for a few minutes with me staring at her and her staring at her desk.

"So..." I begin as she looks up at me and I can see her full lips through that curtain of hair. Very luscious. Very kissable.

"You're not British, are you?" Her question throws me off guard. Out of everything to bring up, she talks about my accent. I mean, where would she even get the impression that I'm not British from? I worked damn hard on this accent!

"What makes ya think?" I can already hear my voice faltering. Damn it.

"Well, other than what you just said a few seconds ago... You slip up. Often actually I can hear a mix between American and British constantly. Don't know how everyone else misses it."

She doesn't even look at me when she says all of this, which is fine because then she won't see my cheeks heat. She's very observant.

"So you've been watching me, huh?" No point in trying to keep up the accent anymore.

"No, there's nothing of interest to watch. I can hear you down the hall or across the campus most of the time. It's not like you try to be quiet." Cracking her fingers, she continues to stare at the top of the desk.

"Ouch. No need to be nice about it." I say, putting a hand to my heart as if wounded. If she truly knew how much I had wanted to see her again, let alone hear her soft voice… just to have her constantly insult me.

"I didn't mean to be rude." She giggles softly and turns her head away. Why does she keep avoiding my gaze?

"I know. I appreciate the honesty though. It's like everyone here is too shallow to speak the truth so they will lie to your face, smiling all the while. It's one thing I can't stand about people."

"Yeah well you've got it easy. Its better they lie to your face then tell you the vicious truth."

"Oh, and what truth are these incompetent college kids saying to you?" Leaning closer I can smell her perfume and I smile knowing it's the same jasmine I smelled before when I held her close.

"If you haven't heard it before you will hear it soon." Her answer is cryptic, but the way she calmly replies really bothers me.

"Why haven't we met before?" Because it's bugging me I can't seem to find her much.

"Because I'm not being seen by you."

"I still should have noticed you."

There's a silence for a few seconds before she speaks again.

"Can I ask you a question?" I smile and nod.

"What are you hiding?" My left eye twitches involuntarily and my fist clenches.

"I don't know what you mean." I say, still trying to smile.

School is the place you go to, to be someone that you're not. It's to do anything you want and never be responsible for anything. It's to be a ghost of your true self. No one needs to know about my skeletons. They're meant to stay in the closet for a reason.

"Why do you do it? The accent I mean. Why fake something like that?"

"Why hide your face?" The question comes out sharper than I intend, and I flinch. "Sorry that was rude."

Arabella sighs before lifting her head and letting her hair fall back.

My first thought is that she's beautiful. Literally beautiful in the purest form of the word. Her lips are even fuller than I thought. I want to kiss them endlessly. And her cheeks are blemish and makeup free, a rarity at this school. Her hair pulled back shapes her face, making her look angelic. I want to kiss every part of her. I want to hear her moans and her cries and feel those lips on my skin. I want her badly. She's gorgeous.

I trace her face from her chin, to her lips and from her lips to her cute nose and then I see her eyes. It's like my heart drops into my stomach and my throat gets dry. Every muscle in my body tenses up at the sight before me and my palms get sweaty. Suddenly I feel like I don't look very good today. The way her eyes are taking me in right now I want to fix my hair and fix my shirt and I just want to look good for her. She's… my God, she's-

"Perfection." Her perfect eyes widen at my choice in description and she blushes again.

"Don't lie. That's cruel." Her words bring me out of the trance her eyes put me in and I smile so wide my cheeks hurt.

"I'm not lying Arabella, I'm being serious. You are the most beautiful girl I have ever seen and trust me I've been around."

"So I've heard." She mutters back. I laugh at that because I had it coming.

"Why would you hide away such striking eyes?" This time Arabella laughs, but it's bitter and short.

"Striking? Beautiful? Perfection? All right, I get it now. This is the real prank. Get the man whore to compliment the freak because he's so popular, and she's so ugly. Have him make up words and spew lies to break down her walls and destroy her from the inside. Because dealing with it daily isn't enough! This place is so full of it. You're all full of it! If you will not be honest, then say nothing. There is nothing good about what you see. It's a deformity! I need to get out of here."

She's up and banging on the door again and it opens to show Lydia and

Jessica walk in with enormous smiles on their faces.

"What's wrong freak can't handle the heat?"

"Oh, my gosh, did he even touch you?"

"If he did, he would have turned into a frog just like her!"

They both laugh, more like cackle, to each other and Arabella pushes past them, hiding her beauty from the world again. Curtaining such wonder from prying eyes. A part of me is glad she does that. I wouldn't want any guy staring at her. She's too pure for them. Too flawless.

Their laughter finally dies down and Lydia wipes a fake tear from her eye.

"Oh Darien we're sorry you had to be in this room with that girl but she totally had it coming the little bitch. All's well that ends well, right? I mean, did you see her? Banging on the door and begging to be out. What a freak. She always was… always will be."

"Yeah she's such a loser." Jessica chimes in. Lydia primps her hair and purses her lips before she smiles at me again.

"Happy Halloween, Darien. I hope to see you at the parties this weekend. And don't worry about trick or treating. I'll be all the treat you need." She kisses my cheek and high fives her friend.

The two of them walk out of the classroom arm in arm still laughing to themselves, leaving me reeling in my seat at everything that just happened. There's so many words, so many emotions still running through my head and yet I can only say one thing.

"Perfection."

Eight

Seriously

Arabella

Church is one of the few places I can admit I enjoy going to. Moving to Anaheim meant finding a new church and finding a new church meant starting fresh and well… who doesn't want a fresh start?

The first Sunday we moved here we visited the Holy House of Praise and learned it was a Pentecostal church. I wasn't the least bit surprised I mean just look at the name! But my parents were a little apprehensive to join the church.

I like to call us church hoppers. I'm sure we've gone to at least five different denominations of Christianity; Anglican, Baptist, Presbyterian, Evangelical, even Orthodox. My parents have never been steadfast on where they worshipped and since we've had to keep moving around due to the bullying, it didn't help either. But entering the Holy House of Praise, something in me just knew I could call this place home.

"The girls are so hot here!" Alec says glancing to a group of girls to our left. I roll my eyes and smile.

"Why don't you focus on the choir song instead of the girls' different colored thon-"

"Arabella just because it rhymes doesn't mean you need to say it." My mother scolds from beside me.

Both Alec and I quietly laugh to ourselves, before paying attention again. It took us coming to this welcoming judgment-free church twice, to know we weren't leaving. Even my parents had made friends while attending here and they can be anti social.

"The girl who's leading the choir couldn't be older than you Ari and yet her voice is so powerful." I turn to Adam to see him staring at the girl like she's some shiny trophy.

Adam's dated a few girls just like the rest of my brothers, but he's much more reserved for the opposite sex. I think it's because he's so sensitive and doesn't enjoy getting hurt.

"She sounds amazing." I reply.

Contrary to popular belief, this isn't an all-black church. There are many white and black people, even some Hispanic and Asian. I like that it's multi-cultured because everyone is different. Skin colour, hair colour, and facial structure, it's all different. And even though I'm not an avid believer in the Almighty anymore, I still enjoy this church more than anything.

"Hey, look Ella that boy is staring at you again." Adrian says smirking. I don't care to look because I know he's lying. The last time he said that was no one there. I won't fall for it again.

"Right." I say, crossing my arms.

I roll my eyes and enjoy the young Hispanic girl finish singing "Take me to the King". The crowd stands up sporadically to cheer her on and praise God, but I remain seated. I know my voice is falling on deaf ears, anyway.

Once she finishes the pastor begins his sermon and I drift off. I already know all the stories and miracles. The past is the past and this Almighty being couldn't change my future.

I zone in and out of the message as the preacher speaks. At one point I stare at the banners on the walls and reconfigure the letters to create extra words. I even count the amount of pews within my sight. I do this often when the preacher gives a sermon.

I hear him shout about redemption and salvation and I nod my head from time to time to make it seem like I'm listening. Such a good fake Christian I am.

As the time goes by the preacher says something that causes the congregation to raise their voices in agreement and clap loudly. Even my family seems really into it. When I finally listen to the message, I hear music play and sigh because the service is coming to a close.

"Wasn't that a great service hun?" I nod towards my mom and smile. She and I both know I'm lying and wasn't paying an ounce of attention, but she stopped calling me on it years ago.

"I really liked that girl's singing. I will see if I can talk to her." Adam says already making his way towards her.

"Hey Bella don't look now but that same guy from before is coming your way." I roll my eyes and push at Alec.

"Jeez you guys can you cut it out? There is no guy comin-" I feel a tap on my shoulder and watch Alec and Adrian's face shine in triumph. Turning around I come face to face with a dark-skinned boy with deep brown eyes and a bright smile. He looks at least a year or two older than me.

"Hi." He's a very good-looking guy... Why is he talking to me?

"Hey." I respond, looking down. What does he want?

"So the sermon was on fire, huh?"

"Yeah it was great."

"Did you like the message?" I nod my head and we stand in silence.

"My name's Benjamin. But you can call me Benji."

"Arabella." I glimpse his smile widening and I smile a little myself.

"That's a beautiful and unique name."

"Thanks, my dad named me."

"He's got great taste." He seems nice, this Benji guy. Much nicer than the kids at school. Much nicer than Darien... Let's see how nice he really is.

I lift my head and meet his eyes and wait for his reaction. His breathing seems to stop and there's a brief twitch near his mouth.

"Oh, wow... Your eyes... That's so different... actually it's unique, just like your name, it suits you." I give him a slight smile and look towards my parents to see them leaving.

"Thank you... Well it was nice meeting you Benji. I guess I'll see you next

In Her Eyes

week." I turn to leave but I feel his hand grip my own and he brings it to his chest... Ok, he could be a psycho or a creep.

"I've been meaning to talk to you since you guys first started coming to this church. I'm so glad I did, you're even more beautiful up close. I'll see you next week, Arabella." I smile and pull my hand back.

I see Adrian just a pew ahead and I latch unto him to get me through the crowd. When I reach the doors, I look towards where we sat and wave to Benji. He grins widely and waves before walking away.

***

"How was your weekend Arabella?" I look up from my book and smile at Vincent.

"Well since I'm the youngest in my family there was no trick or treating so we all just bought lots of food and candy and watched movies. It was fun." Vincent nods and takes a bite from his sandwich.

"Does your family celebrate Halloween?"

"No. The day of the devil and all that. It's no big deal really, I'm not interested in dressing up for a few hours, anyway. No mask can hide who I really am." I mutter that last part because I know Vincent doesn't like it when I degrade myself.

"Yeah, I understand. I used to love Halloween when I was younger. Dressing up and getting all of that candy? And then going to parties with all of those attractive girls. Now I look at my students and shudder. The outfits have gotten shorter and skimpier from what I remember. It's all too much." I laugh and close my book.

"Halloween is just an excuse for girls to dress skanky to catch someone's eye. Not that they don't do it already, but there's a certain *Je ne sais quoi* to a sailor's outfit that regular tights just can't do." Vincent joins in my laughter and we continue to enjoy our lunch.

Nearing the end of my hour and a half lunch break, because I have to have such a long break in between classes, there is a knock on the door and Vincent has to turn down the music.

He looks over to me, a worried expression beginning to grace his features but I smile and signal him to open the door. Even though he can avidly

Seriously

punish the students for bullying me he doesn't enjoy it period. And although I would not eat my lunch elsewhere, Vincent was adamant on me staying in his classroom where he could keep an eye. He's the best.

"Oh, hello Darien am I right? What can I help you with?" How is it possible for this college to be so damn small that he must be everywhere? I could go a month! An entire month without having to deal with him and now I can't get far enough.

"Hey Vince, can I talk to you for a sec?" Vincent leans away from the door and lets Darien in. His eyes land on me immediately and the hard look he seemed to wear easily wipes off.

"Arabella." The way he says my name... breathless and almost relieved... ugh, it makes me want to strangle him all the more.

"Thanks for letting me stay here, Mr. Remington. I'll see you in class tomorrow." I gather my stuff and walk towards the door to leave, yet Darien refuses to move out of my way.

"Arabella... are you ok? With what happened on Friday... I seriously do not understand why they did that. It was just sick."

"I'm fine and I can handle myself. Can you move, please? Unlike most girls I am not getting hot and bothered just being in your presence... I'm just bothered." I raise my head to meet his stare and he gulps before moving out of the way slowly.

"Thank you."

Walking out of the classroom, I glance at my phone and notice I still have ten minutes before my lecture. Great. It's not even like I can go into the hall early because there's already a class in session.

Making my way down the hall and to my left, I aim to go to the library to lose myself in my book again. Glancing at the door, I pull it open only to have to shut closed again.

"You walk much faster than you look."

Deep breaths, Ari. Deep breaths. No need to strangle this annoying pest of a boy. He just wants to get in your pants, and you won't let him. Just be polite.

"Why did you follow me?" I ask, my voice coming out steadier than I feel.

That same cologne from the last time I bumped into him is floating in the air between us and I can't help taking in a discreet whiff of it. Why does he have to smell so good?

"I just wanted to know that you were ok." Something in my chest jumps and I scowl.

"I already told you I can handle myself. Can you leave me alone?" Darien smiles down at me stuffs his hands in his pockets.

"You're so feisty and stubborn. I guess you have to be huh?" Looking into his eyes I know he isn't trying to be rude, but it doesn't mean what he's saying... how he's looking at me doesn't bother me.

"Yeah well when you have a deformity like mine you learn to be tough." I turn on my heels and begin walking to my next class. *No more book for me.* I can hear Darien keeping pace beside me and I groan and stop to face him again.

"Seriously?" I ask, gritting my teeth. He smiles wide again and shrugs.

"Seriously." What a stupid answer from a stupid boy. I just keep walking.

My class isn't too far away and seeing the students filing out of the lecture hall makes me want to dance. I reach the door and I practically run in and sit in my seat at the back. Darien laughs and walks in, causally saluting a student a row in front of me before sitting on the desk beside me.

"You know you're pretty when you're angry." His comment makes me shudder in disgust.

"Is that seriously all you've got? Do you use that pathetic line on every girl or just the ones you find lacking?" His eyes widen at my comment and so do my own.

Why did I just say that? That was like putting a "Come on in" sign on my forehead. He'll never leave me alone now!

"There is nothing you're lacking, Arabella." The depth to those words is as shallow as the kiddie pool my dad bought me when I was five.

"Don't you have someone else to harass?" Annoyance coats my every word.

Why must he bother me out of everyone in this blasted college? Seeing him three times in almost two months is enough torture for me. Why can't he leech on to someone who wants to be in his presence?

"I wouldn't consider my flirting to be harassment. That is a first."

"Yeah well not everyone is so keen on your charm."

"So, you think I'm charming?" I swear his face will crack with how wide he's smiling right now. The jerk.

"Why won't you leave me alone?"

"Why won't you say my name?"

"Huh?" He bends down to my height. His green eyes piercing right through me and suddenly I feel vulnerable.

"Say my name." His mouth is so close to mine and his smile is mocking me. Taunting me. Daring me to run again. The jerk.

"Why?" His lips curve up and he leans closer.

"Say my name." He thinks this is a game. He thinks I'm one of those flaky, desperate girls just vying for his attention. He's wrong.

"No." Darien's eyes squint and his jaw clenches, but his smirk remains.

"Say my name."

"Get out of my class, you man whore." Again, his lips curve up, his smile getting bigger and bigger.

"Say my name Arabella." Again, that weird thump in my chest.

"Man whore." He licks his lips and leans closer to me. His voice no louder than before, but somehow, it's become the only sound I can hear.

"Say. My. Name." There's something in the way he's looking at me. Something in the way I can feel myself slowly leaning into him. Something in the electricity that's crackling between us. Something that making my stomach woozy.

And just like that, I take notice of the scene we have created. I didn't hear the murmurs of people. I didn't see the students file in. And I didn't notice everyone's eyes on us. Just like that, my anger and annoyance turns, into embarrassment. I let my hair fall forward as I shrink into my seat and look away.

"Darien." I whisper out.

I don't have to see his face to know he's disappointed. He was enjoying toying with me. Just like everyone else. This boy is no different. The sooner I learn that, the better.

Nine

I'm a Horny Confused Idiot

Darien

This past weekend has been the most unnerving I've ever had to endure. It's like ever since Friday every part of me has been alive and thrumming and craving something that I know I probably could never have. Arabella.

After she left me in that classroom, I found I still couldn't move. Her beauty, her voice, her hair… her everything had me ensnared the moment she looked me in the eye.

And damn, her eyes are amazing. They're a wonder. They're wonderful. She's wonderful. I mean two unique eye colours? That's so different and marvelous and perfect and that makes her special and so damn pretty. Her right eye is crystal blue, and her left eye a gorgeous hazel… Damn.

So getting through two days without having a clue where to find her drove me stir crazy. I haven't had a crush on a girl since I was ten and here I am ten years later and I'm still the hopeless fool I remembered myself to be. Daydreaming about her every other second of the day.

I tried finding her on *Facebook, Twitter, Instagram, Snapchat, Vine, Kik, What's App, BBM* and I found nothing! Can you imagine? Not a damn thing! Does she not know what social media is? Does she shun technology? Does she not realize I am frantic to see even a glimpse of her to get me through the day!

I thought about just asking around about her but I knew the results I would get would be rude, offensive and negative. So instead I figured I'd have to wait until Tuesday.

I spent those three days doing everything I could to keep my mind off of her until I could see her again. The only thing I know can easily distract me is sex, and I had a lot.

It was Halloween so everyone was having a party and at every party there are at least three girls more than willing to get with me because they want to know if I'm as good as everyone says I am or to show off to their friends. Most times I would prefer not to play games in such a manner as jealousy or spite, but I took whatever I could get.

Hooking up with those girls... it made it easier not to dwell on the fact that I've been wanting to kiss Arabella's lips the moment I saw them. Or that her hair smells and looks like it was in a Herbal Essence commercial. Or that I'm sure, even though she acts shy, that she is a freak in the sheets. And then as I continued to thrust into those faceless girls, I imagined what it would be like to be with Arabella sexually.

I'd never been so turned on by rejection before. But I've never faced rejection before either, so what do I know? Twice she's turned me away and I still want to go back to her like an idiot. A horny, confused idiot. I know she's most likely pushing me away because of the abuse she's received from those insecure bimbos at school. I can understand her pain and hurt. I can get that she may never want to see me again, but I don't think I can stay away. Hell, I don't want to. There's so much about her that piques my curiosity. She makes me feel... like myself again and it's been a long time since I've felt like that.

"Tell me man, wasn't that party crazy last night?" Matt whispers beside me.

"Nothing I haven't seen before." I reply and stare down at my textbook.

Ms. Lopez is teaching something new in calculus today, but I can't focus. I know Arabella has a class with Lydia and Jessica right now because they blabbed it to me yesterday. So right now, she's learning how to write, because that's what they do in Writer's Craft, right?

And then she'll be on her way to some Shakespeare class and I know this because I've seen her schedule. The rest of the day I am completely at a loss but this school isn't that big so I know I'll be able to find her eventually. Should be easy.

***

What the absolute hell! Where is she? How can she be off the map? I know she hasn't left school property because someone would have told me by now. I have people watching all the doors. And she's not in the commons area, nor is she outside. I checked the writing labs and the library and nothing! I even told some girls to check the bathrooms, and she's nowhere.

"Hey, can you give me a ride to-"

"No, I'm busy."

"But you're just standing there." I turn to Matt and narrow my eyes.

"I said I'm busy." Stalking off to Vince Remington's class, I decide maybe he can help me. I heard he is the only teacher with a stationary class because he refused to leave it. The guy is a legend. He practically knows everyone here, so he should at least know Arabella.

His door is slightly ajar, so I knock on it and wait for him to answer. I can hear some music playing in there and he looks chill with his feet up on his desk. As he turns down what sounds like classical music, I bounce from foot to foot. He opens the door and I smile lightly.

"Oh, hello Darien. What can I help you with?" This guy is probably a lady killer with a smile like his.

"Hey Vince, can I talk to you for a sec?" He moves to the side and I casually step in. Something alerts me to my right, a sound almost like a squeak and I turn to see Arabella at a desk with her lunch set up and a book on the table. I can feel myself visibly relax at the sight of her.

"Arabella." Saying her name like that… oh God what she can do to my body with just the sight of her. She glances me sharply and gathers her things. Her hands are fumbling, and she keeps blowing her hair out of her face and she's just adorable.

"Thanks for letting me stay here, Mr. Remington. I'll see you tomorrow." I watch her walk towards me and I realize she wants to leave. Ha. She's not going anywhere yet. Not until I talk to her some more. Just to at least make sure she's ok. Lydia can be the devil when she wants to, and what she did to Arabella was cruel.

"Arabella… are you ok? With what happened on Friday… I seriously do not understand why they did that. It was just sick." Her face grimaces at the memory before she steels her spine.

"I'm fine and I can handle myself. Can you move, please? Unlike most girls, I am not getting hot and bothered just being in your presence… I'm just bothered." Her head lifts to meet my eyes, and it hits me square in the gut. The gulp that follows is involuntary and I decidedly move out of her way. She's so brave and so strong.

"Thank you." I watch her walk out of the room with the grace of royalty and I realize that there is no way she would ever go for me. I don't have a chance-

"So, you're smitten with her too, huh? I've noticed some guys watching her when they think no one is looking. But no one has shown their infatuation. Probably out of fear of Lydia. Arabella's a special girl, that's for sure. And very talented. The best student I've had to date…"

I don't stay any longer to hear Vince's spiel because he's said guys have been watching her. As in watching her like they want her. As in, they think they can have a shot with her.

I shouldn't feel so possessive over a girl I hardly know. I should definitely walk away before I'm in too deep. There are a lot of things I should do, but instead I catch her walking towards the library, and I rush to close the door before she enters.

"You walk much faster than you look." Leaning over her like this, being so close to her even when I can tell she's agitated, it feels wrong. Wrong because I'm feeling something more than fleeting emotions. I'm feeling things I've tried to bury away. It's wrong, but it's so good.

"Why did you follow me?" A simple question really, and yet if she really knew then she'd never give me the time of day. So, let's go with the oblivious card.

"I just wanted to know that you were ok." She scowls. *Man, this girl won't give in.*

"I already told you I can handle myself. Can you leave me alone?" *Yes, I could leave you alone but the actual question is do I want to?* I smile to myself at the thought and rest my hands in my pockets.

"You're so feisty and stubborn. I guess you have to be, huh?" She finally looks up at me and I suck in a breath. She's just stunning.

"Yeah well when you have a deformity like mine you learn to be tough."

Why does she keep saying a deformity? What does she think is wrong with her? She spins away from me and goes back down the hall, probably to her next class. I'm following right beside her, causing her to stop and groan.

"Seriously?" I smile at her like a goofball. A flashback of a younger me, just as eager, just as desperate reels in my head, but I push the memory away.

"Seriously." Her jaw clenches as she continues to move forward.

I watch her stealthily maneuver through the hordes of students to her next class. *You haven't lost me that easily.* Laughing, I walk into the lecture hall with her and wave to the student organizing his desk ahead of us. He looks shocked to see me. Arabella's seat is all the way at the back of the hall, so I sit at the empty desk beside her.

"You know you're pretty when you're angry." What a stupid, stupid line. *Come on Darien, you're better than that!*

"Is that seriously all you've got? Do you use that pathetic line on every girl or just the ones you find lacking?" Ouch! That comment is harsh and sexy all in one.

"There is nothing you're lacking, Arabella." *And I will damn well make sure I prove that to you.*

"Don't you have someone else to harass?" Her annoyance is getting very apparent now. *Good, let's play with it.*

"I wouldn't consider my flirting to be harassment. That is a first."

"Yeah well not everyone is so keen on your charm."

"So, you think I'm charming?" Her face heats and my smile widens.

"Why won't you leave me alone?"

"Why won't you say my name?"

"Huh?" I watch the confusion spread across her face and I know I've gotten to her. Bending down to her height, I look into her eyes and almost get lost.

"Say my name."

"Why?" I lean in closer to her and smell her hair, it's tropical and sweet and I want to stick my face in it and smell her all day.

"Say my name."

"No." *That's right, fight me. Keep fighting me, Arabella. I love a challenge.*

"Say my name."

"Get out of my classroom, you man whore." *So sexy.*

"Say my name, Arabella."

"Man whore." The amount of things I want to do to this girl right now is making me more aroused than ever. Making me want her more than breathing. Making me want to claim her right here, right now for all these annoying people to see.

"Say. My. Name." I watch as she unconsciously leans forward, causing me move closer to her. Her full delicious lips are right there. So close to my own. I want to bite them. But something in her changes.

It's like she somehow wakes up and her eyes jump around to the faces watching us. I can see it. I can see her shrinking back into the shell that these monsters have put her in. I can see her hide herself away and suddenly I want to stop her.

I want to shake her and beg her to stay with me. To fight me. To do something other than hide. But she doesn't and I don't know why she makes me feel this way. It's terrifying and invigorating.

"Darien."

Her voice is so quiet and so weak coming out of those precious lips. This isn't a game between us anymore and it's not a challenge. Hell, it's not even a fight anymore. This is a war between me, Arabella and those punks that have dragged her down.

I will be her savior.

I will pull her out of that darkness.

And I will make her mine fears be damned.

Ten

No... Ok Maybe

Arabella
Darien's waiting for me when I finish class. I turn to my left to see him leaning against the wall next to me, just casually typing away on his phone. Walking past him and I try to blend in with the crowd, but he isn't fooled. He stays right beside me all the way to my mother's car. The creep even watches me as we drive away. He doesn't move from his spot until I'm out of sight. It's like he's rooted to it.

I asked my mom about the telltale signs of stalking. She didn't take me seriously, but I was being dead serious.

The next day Darien repeated his odd actions. He was there for Vince's class and he joined Vince and me for lunch and then he walked me to my mom's car again and watched me drive away. What bothered me more than him following me, were the flock of sheep that followed him. His presence was magnetic, drawing everyone in and causing surprise and annoyance when they saw me.

We spent the first week not talking at all. I didn't want to say anything to him because I knew it would encourage him. I thought if I kept quiet the entire time, he would eventually get bored with me and move on. I was wrong.

The second week I argued with him. I called him plenty of cruel names and told him to go where his skanks were, but he laughed and kept following. The flock thought it was funny to see me yell at him. I tried to call him every mean name I'd known, including the ones that The Almighty wouldn't approve of and he still wouldn't budge. The flock laughed and teased him for taking it, but he remained by my side the entire time.

I remember hiding out in the girl's bathroom for twenty minutes. Some girls stared at me, while others said someone who looks like me would never deserve him. They were right but when I came out, he was leaning against the wall next to me, the flock hovering close by.

Some would call this a romantic gesture, I call it crazy. It was like every day he would smile at me and say my name softly, like a purr coming from his mouth. His eyes would watch my every movement and I could tell he was analyzing me, as if he was looking for something. I don't know why he started this new… thing, but I couldn't get rid of him. And when the flock realized he wasn't leaving either they began to get bored of us.

One by one they fell away, more annoyed that I was monopolizing his unwanted time, than upset with him for acknowledging my existence. The guys had strange looks in their eyes, as if they were trying to see something more from me than what I was showing. When Darien's attention wasn't on me, the girls would leer and say I'm too dark, or my hair is too unruly for Darien's tastes as if they were speaking for the man himself. It's nothing I'd never heard before, but for the first time it hurt deeper than it usually did. I tried my hardest to ignore the feeling.

The third week the weather was getting colder. It was late November and though there wasn't any snow, there were chilly days. I remember there being so much snow in New York when I lived there as a child. I loved watching it fall from the sky and dust the streets and cars. It's different here. In Anaheim they put up fake snow designs and buy trees with artificial snow to replace the actual thing.

When I mistakably complained about wanting something hot to drink in the mornings, Darien brought me different drinks to warm me up. What was remaining of the flock wanted his attention too, yet he smiled them off.

He never openly rejected them, merely ignored their presence. They never got the hint.

Monday it was coffee. Tuesday it was a latte. Wednesday it was a cappuccino. Thursday it was hot apple cider. Friday it was a chai tea latte. Damn him because I love chai tea and I couldn't help the moan that escaped me when I tasted the Oprah's Chai tea blend, he bought me from Starbucks. That day he was overly happy, and I regretted ever opening my mouth. If the looks from the flock could kill, I'd be dead ten times over.

I always paid him back around five dollars to make sure I never owed him a cent but then he'd use that money to buy my next drink. He seemed so proud of himself for finding out something that made me happy and I don't know why.

What surprised me more was the conflict that warred on his face when he thought I wasn't looking. His forehead would wrinkle and his jaw would tighten causing a vein to appear on his left temple. It looked like he was fighting with himself. It only lasts a few moments and he's always able to school his features back into that soft smile.

As the days went by even the flock could see it was obvious I didn't like him and wished he would waste his time somewhere else, but he didn't seem to get it. All he did was smile and flash me those emerald eyes, making me want to punch him and then maybe hug him.

By the fourth week we became a little more civil. The flock had all but dispersed, only giving a meager, yet still flirtatious "Hi" when we walked by. I stopped calling him nasty names and talked to him a little nicer.

He continued to buy me chai tea lattes every morning and told me about the lame parties he's gone to over the years. Some of his stories were actually funny and I couldn't stop myself from laughing at them. He's really good at illuminating each moment..

The differences in his character with me and with the flock became more apparent. He'd have the tendency of tensing up when around them, forcing a smile that looked too tight and acting so… fake. While with me, he seemed relaxed and a little down. Like he was enjoying my company but also worried about us getting too close.

I have to admit I enjoyed the fourth week of his stalking the most. I realized that being friendly with him made life so much easier. His smile made me smile. His laugh made me laugh. His eyes sparkled, and I stared into them like a creep. He pulled me further and further into his cheerful persona and I was finder it harder to get out. But I made sure he didn't know it. I continued to hate him on the outside and adore him on the inside.

***

December has finally come, and the semester is almost over. Tests and assignments have been piling up and so has the bullying, not that I'm surprised.

When I was being bullied before I would just hide away and block out the world. The only thing people could use against me was my looks. But now that one of the most gorgeous guys on campus won't leave me alone, people have been noticing me a little too much. Sure the flock is gone, but they're still talking.

The bickering between Lydia and Jessica has become incessant and their words have become crueler. They've grown the alien hyenas pack to spite and follow me around everywhere I go.

I'm guessing they recruited all of Darien's scorned lovers to go against me. There are at least ten of them now. And they all hate me. I could handle it just being my deformity, but now that it involves a guy, a guy I want nothing to do with no less... Now things are much more complicated.

"What's on your mind teleiótita?" As of late Darien has taking a liking to that word. Every time I ask him what it means he just smiles and says I already know. The jerk.

"You should leave me alone." He smiles... I hate his smile, it makes his eyes brighten... I hate his eyes too.

"Uh, huh. Did you like your latte this morning? If you're tiring of it I'm sure there's something els-"

"I'm serious, Darien. You need to leave me alone." I say as sternly as I can.

He stops walking and steps in front of me, his head tilting to the side. His eyes search my face for something before he frowns and his jaw clenches. The vein appears on his temple again.

"Who is it?" His voice is hard and annoyed, and I bite my lip. The change in his demeanor could make me laugh. He eyes the subtle grind of my teeth against my skin with ferocious focus. I'd stop if I cared to, but he's openly ogled me so much I'm used to it.

"Who is what?" I ask timidly.

"Don't play dumb teleiótita someone is bothering you. I can see it. You accepted me," he gestures to the space in between us, "us, weeks ago. So, who is bothering you?" I bite the inside of my cheek. I never accepted him. I just grew… accustomed to him. Something that looks akin to fear flashes in his eyes before it disappears.

"It's not really… I mean, I can handle it. I'm just saying there's no rhyme or reason to why this," I copy his gesture, "should happen in the first place. We aren't a couple, we aren't friends, we're just-"

"What we are we can discuss when you're ready to talk about it. What matters is that we deal with whoever is bothering you now. So, either you tell me who it is or I will start following you in class and out of class."

My eyes widen at that because somewhere deep down I know he isn't joking. But I'm not some weakling who needs protecting from some stupid catty girls. I can fight my own battles… By not engaging in the to being with.

"It's none of your concern Darie-"

"All right following you in it is." He leads the way ahead of me towards my Stage and Screen Writing class.

He literally has no other classes for the day so he could very well follow me into class and sit with me the entire time. Three out of the eleven alien hyenas are in this class. All of them he's slept with. This should be good.

When I walk into the lecture hall, I see him sitting at the desk beside my usual. He looks comfortable and agitated all at once. The alien hyenas are already here and they're immediately all over him. Good, that way they can leave me alone.

Sitting down, I take out my script and notebook and prepare myself for the class. The teacher walks in and glances up at Darien before shaking his head and beginning the class. I try my hardest to focus on the lesson as I know we have exams coming soon, but I can't help wondering what Darien is doing. I can see him from the corner of my eye whispering something to the alien hyenas and they're laughing in return.

He's probably telling them how pathetic you are for hanging off of him like you do.

The voice of Lydia fills my head and I groan. Darien hears it.

"Teleiótita are you alright?" He brings his chair closer to mine and takes my hand. We've never touched before. It was like an unspoken rule between us. Sure, he'd be beside me almost all the time, but we never touched, because touching would mean something different in our strange dynamic. Besides, I'm sure he'd find me very mature if I told him "no touchy".

"I'm fine." I whisper back to him. He doesn't believe me. He's never satisfied. He just won't leave me alone.

Conflict wars on his face as his hand squeezes mine, but he doesn't let go. In fact, it's been thirty-two scratch that, thirty-three seconds since he first touched my hand and he's still touching it. Touching me.

His hands are soft and warm. I can smell the moisturizer on his skin. There's a light tracing of hair in the middle of his hand, leading up his arm. He's not hairy either... I like that. I should tell him to let go of my hand. I should pull away, and yet...

"Why are you touching her?" I pull my hand back. Darien looks between me, and the alien hyenas beside him before understanding hits his green eyes.

"Because I want to touch her. Do you have a problem with that? Not that it's any of your business. Why don't you ladies pay attention to your teacher? This is an important review."

His hand reaches for mine again, but I keep it under my desk.

No touchy. I think to myself.

***

"What are you doing for Christmas holidays Arabella?" Darien asks as he sits with me in Vince's class. He's been here every day for lunch. The flock used to join us some days, not anymore.

"Not sure yet." I answer quietly.

He smiles (did I mention I hate that smile) and takes my hand. He's been touching my hand ever since my class last week. He only does it when I'm watching him. He's slow to do it, always cautious.

"Can I spend the holidays with you?"

"No." The answer is immediate, and Vince laughs out loud before covering it up with a cough.

No. No. No. No. No... maybe.

"I don't mean meeting the family... though technically I've already met everyone except your mother." I roll my eyes and he laughs.

"No."

No. No. No. No... maybe.

"What about one day?"

"No."

No. No. No... maybe.

The pout on his face is both adorable and sexy and I want to lick him suddenly. I'm sure he'd taste like sin... and candy.

"Ok half a day?"

"No."

He licks his lip. Damn that lip. Damn him. He's too attractive for his own good. Too damn attractive.

No. No... maybe.

"Ok... a few hours! I'll make it the best few hours of your life!" I raise my eyebrow at that, and he blushes. Darien never blushes. He's too damn cocky to blush. This time Vince doesn't hold back his laughter.

"Sorry I mean... not that. Of course, not that. But if you want to-"

"No." The blush gets deeper on his tanned skin. "Don't even go there."

"Right. But I meant it. They could be an exceptional few hours teleiótita." I sigh and go back to picking at my salad.

"Are you ever going to tell me what that means?" I mutter.

Darien perks up like a puppy about to receive a treat.

"I'll tell you if you let me have those hours."

"No."

No... ok maybe...

"Don't you want to know what it means?"

"It's Greek I've figured out that much." His eyes widen in surprise before he leans towards me.

"Then you want to know." He's such a pain.

"I never said I didn't."

"Give me those hours, teleiótita." He's too tempting and evil and sexy and wicked.

"How many hours?" There he goes, licking that accursed lip again.

"Nine."

"Two."

"Eight."

"Two."

"Seven."

"Two."

"Six and that's as low as I'll go."

Six hours alone with the ex-British man whore…

"Deal."

Eleven

The Devil on My Shoulder

Darien

I've never had a problem with tests. Their easy. Exams, too. I find if you don't over think and stress then the test is easier than it looks. It's worked like a charm for me. Arabella is a whole other situation.

"Why are you still here? GO away!" She keeps nibbling on her lip and her hair is a mess and not a sexy mess like I like it either. I don't think she's slept much this week.

She hasn't been this upset since our first week. She's nervous. Her Shakespeare test is apparently hard. She's been studying every day after class and skipping lunch. She's freaking out. I want to help her and then kiss her, but then I want to run and revert back to my old self so I can stop feeling so helpless around her. It's a warzone in my head.

"I have nothing to do right now so let me help you." She shakes her head repeatedly and turns away.

"You have class. Go to it. Or go have sex with someone. Be of use somewhere else." *I'd love to have sex with you. Repeatedly. Night and day. Non-stop. Hot and sweaty and hard and fast and-*

"What are you staring at so hard?" I look up to Arabella's face and grimace. I was looking at her breasts. I didn't mean to, but she's the one who had

The Devil on My Shoulder

to bring up sex. I haven't had sex in three weeks. And for someone like me, that's a long time.

"Nothing. Sorry. Let me help you. I thought we were friends." Arabella cuts her eyes to me.

"We aren't friends. I don't know what we are or why you keep bothering me." I haven't exactly told her the reason either.

"I'm not bothering you." I say defensively.

"Yes, you are Darien. Now shoo!"

She makes a motion with her hands and I take one in mine. I love touching her. I can feel her pulse race every time I do. Which means whether she acknowledges it or not, I excite her and that excites me. I've missed feeling this free with my emotions. Kind of.

"Are you excited for our six hours together?" Her pulse skips a beat. She's excited.

"No. I need to study Darien, please go." I pout and let go of her hand.

I hate seeing her stressed. I prefer her feisty and observant. I like it when she tries not to like me. I loved it when she shared her lunch with me three days ago. It was a club sandwich. I hate sandwiches, but I ate it, anyway.

"All right I'll go…" I take my time leaving trying to be as dramatic as possible but she's not paying me an ounce of attention. I'm such a loser. I need to get a grip. This is not who I've created myself to be. I need to loosen up.

"Bye." Short, curt and dismissive. That's how she's been lately. Maybe she's tiring of me. That wouldn't surprise me, I am being needy. I feel a vibration in my pocket and take out my phone.

Mel 2: Are you busy?

I want to respond, yes. I want to tell her I'm not interested, and I'm taken and may never be single again if I can help it. But I don't.

Darien: You need something? *You know what you need, Darien. The one thing that can get your mind off anything and your body onto anyone. The one thing that feels too good to ignore. You've been craving it.*

Mel 2: You. *Three weeks is a long time.*

I can see the devil on my shoulder polishing his pitchfork and pulling out a box of condoms. He's parading around his territory in his boxers and doing some crunches to help define his six-pack. He's evil and horny... and I'm... I shouldn't. I should just go home and take a cold shower like I always do...

Darien: Your place or mine? *Yes! Free yourself, Darien! Get some action! Use one girl–no! NO! Use two! We need TWO!*

Mel 2: Mine.

She doesn't live that far from here and I need not go to class since I already have the exam review. I could make it quick and be back for the bell.

Darien: Be there in 10 and bring a friend.

I haven't had a threesome in a few months. It will keep me fit and relieve me for at least another week. Besides...

What Arabella doesn't know won't hurt us.

***

So, the sex was much longer than I thought it would be, but damn did it feel good. These two girls were complete and utter freaks in. We ended up going at it until the evening.

Mel said it was the best she's had in a while and her friend was too tired to speak. But showing up on campus today, I keep getting high fives and winks from people. Someone must have blabbed about yesterday which is fine... just as long as Arabella doesn't hear about it then I'm all good.

Class is short and sweet, just as I like it. We thankfully have no exams in my intro to communications class, so we're finished for the semester... meaning more time to spend with Arabella.

I head to Vince's class a few minutes late since Taylor wanted the details to my ménage à trois after class. Walking in I feel cold suddenly and I don't really know how to explain it.

"Why are you here?" Her voice is distant even though she's only a few feet away from me.

Arabella is sitting in her usual spot at the back of the class with her head down as she stabs at her lunch. She's mad. But she doesn't know. She can't know. It was with two girls that she doesn't even know. And since when did she listen to the rumor mill?

"I always eat lunch with you." I say as nonchalantly as possible. I take my seat beside her and notice Vince is eerily quiet in front.

Oh yeah, she knows.
"You should leave."

"I will stay. I didn't see you all morning, so your latte is cold. Sorry." I hand it to her, and she takes it.

"You should leave." I force a laugh and eat my bag of chips. Memories of a desperate young boy keep flashing in my mind. I try to push them back but the fear pushes them forward.

"You ready for exams tomorrow?"

"You should leave." I sigh and put down my food. I already know what's coming. It's happened before. It's what I've been trying to avoid. My mind is whirling with too many emotions. It's hard to keep a straight face.

"Arabella pleas–"

"You should leave."

"Ok what's wrong? I left you like you asked and had sex. So what? You said to have sex! What did you expect me to do when you were being so cold?" Arabella rolls her eyes and gets up. I think she will leave, but she dumps the tea in the trash.

"You should leave." *Ok, now I'm pissed.* I can't get a hold my emotions, they're starting to slip past my control.

"Talk to me!" Her head whips around and I notice Vince has left the classroom.

"Talk to you? Talk to you and say what?" I've never seen her so angry before. It's like staring at a hurricane and feeling it's force. She's beautifully terrifying, and she's going to tear me apart.

"I don't know! Are you mad? Are you sad? What the hell is going on up there?" She shakes her head and stays away from me.

"I can't believe you would have sex with two girls at once!"

"But you told me to!"

"Are you seriously that dense?"

"No, I'm not, but when the girl I care about is constantly rejecting me and pushing me away then what else am I to do, huh? You want me to fight for you? I fight for you! You want me to protect you? I protect you. You want me to leave you alone and yet your eyes, your heartbeat, your body say differently."

"Shut up." A weak defense. *She's losing ground and I'm moving in. I can't lose her. Not again.*

"No, I won't shut up. Ok yes, I had a threesome with some girls. Yes, I wished it was you the entire time. Yes, I wish we could move past this damn friendship and be something more! Yes, I just... I don't know!"

"We aren't friends, we aren't anything. We should cut our losses now. It was fun, and you were kind, but it made no sense. It never will. Leave me be and go be you. I knew the whole celibacy act couldn't last long. I knew you were just like the rest of them." She says walking away from me.

It's happening again. She's shrinking back into that shell. She's locking me out. What the hell! I had made progress! *And you screwed up just like before. It will always come back full circle Darien.*

"No! Why now? Why not weeks ago?"

"I tried weeks ago, but you thought it was a joke! Well, I'm not joking anymore. This is over. You can't be trusted. Whatever this was..."

"Don't push me away Arabella. We don't need a label. We are just us. I enjoy being us. Can't we just stay as us?" Her eyes, her face, her everything... my teleiótita looks away from me. She's shut me out again.

"There was never an us."

***

"I hate the holidays." I say to my parents as we eat this crappy Christmas dinner. My mom looks up with concern and stops eating.

"Sweetheart you love Christmas. I remember when you were younger-"

"That was then. This is now." I need to shut away my emotions again. I have to because I hate everything and I hate nothing and I want Arabella back so badly.

I don't understand what it is about her. In comparison to the last girl she's her opposite. I barely even know the girl and yet I am hooked on her. Being with her was addicting. Listening to her voice, smelling her perfume, touching her skin, all of it was addicting. And it's made me crave her and worst of all... it's made me miss her.

I've never felt so depressed... not since. I snap myself out of those thoughts and focus on Arabella instead.

I want to go back to a week and a half ago and tell myself not to take up Melinda's offer. I want to throw myself at Arabella's feet and kiss the ground she walks on because she's so strong and I'm nothing more than a coward.

"Son is this about that girl?" My head pops up.

"What girl?" Mom smiles and looks to dad, who's smirking.

"You've been spelling out her name with your peas for the past half hour." I look down to my plate and there it is. Variations of her name on my plate spelled out with peas and mashed potatoes. Ari, Belle, and Arabella.

"Oh... I didn't mean to."

"Yes, well when you're in love, those things can happen." Love... I can't be in love with her. I mean... can I? I barely even know the girl. It's not love, that's ridiculous.

"I'm not in love with her. I just like her." Mom stifles a laugh and looks at my plate.

"Well, tell me about this Ari girl." *No, because if I talk about her then I will miss her more and I can't stand to be any more pathetic than I am now.*

"I'd rather not." My parents share a look again and nod.

They eat the rest of dinner in silence and I avoid my food altogether.

***

Matt: New Year's party tonight! You're coming, right?

I roll my eyes at his text and leave the phone on my nightstand. I don't want to go anywhere. I don't want to do anything. Well, I want to do Arabella but that may never happen now. I wish I was smart enough to ask for her number. *Wait... her number!* I grab my notebook and scroll through the pages.

For the past few weeks, we had been playing a game of whether I could guess her cell number. She would write out three numbers and I'd guess which one was a part of the three digits for each part for her cell. Scrolling through the pages, I find the game and write out six different variations of her phone number. I call each one, praying to anyone out there that she answers. And each one is a bust. But I try them all over again. And again. And again. Till someone answers.

"Hello?"

"Teleiótita?"

"Darien? How did you get my number?" I am so lucky right now.

"Our game, remember?" There's no response and I think she's hung up.

"I forgot about that."

"I almost did too... so how've you been?" Again silence.

"Fine. I should go."

"Wait! Can I still have my six hours?" She scoffs and I hear some static.

"As if that applies to you anymore."

"How many times must I say I'm sorry?"

"It doesn't matter Darie-"

"I'm sorry."

"What?"

"I'm sorry."

"Darien stop."

"I'm sorry. I'm so sorry. I'm sorry I messed up. I'm sorry I gave in. I'm sorry I didn't think straight. I'm sorry I hurt you-"

"You didn't hurt me-"

"I'm sorry I'm an idiot. I'm sorry for saying sorry so many times. I'm sorry-"

"All right! all right! Enough! You can have your six hours. God." I don't think I've smiled so hard in my life but the fear gnaws at my mind. The darkness I'd been living in demanding to remain.

Run, Darien, don't go back to her. Don't fall deeper. Forcing myself to ignore those thoughts I focus on the alleviation of the striking pain in my chest.

"Can it be now? Are you busy tonight? I know it's New Year's Eve and all." She sucks in a breath and I hold my own.

"My family doesn't do much celebrating wise so if that means it will be over with then yes." My heart is beating so hard I need to hold my chest. The images are flashing again, the eager boy beggin for attention.

"Text me your address and I'll be there in twenty minutes." Arabella, my teleiótita, sighs and hangs up.

Six hours to change her mind. Six hours to change her heart. Six hours to completely forget.

Twelve

God Let Me Hate Him a Little

Arabella

It's been a confusing couple of months. I never figured going to college would open the door to a guy liking me. I'm surprised that I'm liked by someone other than a teacher. Because it's obvious that Darien likes me. I don't know why but he does. It makes me feel so self-conscience. I'd never had an issue with my body, only my looks yet with Darien, with the excessive stares, I feel so exposed. My hair feels scratchy instead of soft, like it's too full, too obvious too… Black. My skin seems darker and making my eyes stand out even more. My breasts, what little I have of them seem worthless bags of fat compared to other girls, which they kind of are. Everything is different and it's all his fault.

Maybe this is all a part of our plan. He acts like he cares about you and then he exposes you for the freak you are. Let's face it, no one could ever feel anything more than remorse for a face like yours.

Lydia's voice snickers in my mind. She's becoming a permanent nuisance up there. She's pushing me further and further away from the happiness that I want but I know I don't deserve. I don't know what I did in life to have such a snide tormentor but there she is; plumped up lips and evil eyes laughing at me and calling me names I already call myself. Maybe deep down Lydia is my motivator to stay the same. There's no need to change myself because no one will ever see me for more than my deformity any way.

"Are you coming down Ari?" I hear Adam's voice outside my door and zip up my sweater. I haven't told my family that I will spend the next six hours with a boy that has some sick need to act like someone he's not. I should really figure out why he faked that stupid accent, eventually. I mean, I can't believe people fell for that. It was so fake it made Barbie look real.

"No, I'm going out with a friend." The silence that ensues makes Lydia cackle. She knows that no one would want to spend time with me. She knows that I should keep myself hidden away. She knows…

"Really? Who with?" My heart races as Adam opens the door.

His face is curious and cautious as he lingers in the doorway. I don't have many friends, if it wasn't obvious before, so I'm not surprised by his reaction.

"Some guy from school." His eyebrows shoot into his hairline and he pales.

"Like… Like a…" He gulps and runs a shaky hand through his hair, "Date?"

Rolling my eyes I grab my bag, wallet and phone. I leave my hair out and wear no make-up; I don't want Darien thinking this is anything more than it is… whatever this is.

"No, it's not a date. Not even close to a date. I just owe this guy a favor I guess and he wants to spend it today. I will be home in six hours." Adam closes the door behind him and crosses his arms.

"Six hours! He can't be that good!" My mouth drops open and we both blush at what he just said. IS HE CRAZY?

"We are not having sex, Adam! I–I don't know what we're doing but we're not doing that!" Warily Adam comes to sit on my bed.

"Then why are you going? Is he forcing you to do this?" I look away and clutch my sheets.

I don't know why I'm doing this… why I'm even giving him a second chance after he acted like such a man whore!

"No. No, I agreed to this. It's just… we had a fight and… I just don't know anymore. He's so-" The doorbell rings and we both jump. I look at my alarm clock and see he's five minutes early. I can't do this. I grip Adam's arm and cringe when the bell rings again.

"I–I can't–I can't do this." He looks down at me and nods before leaving the room.

Seconds pass and I hear nothing. Staring at the clock only two minutes have gone by but it feels like hours. Hopefully Adam sends him away with a death glare or something scary to shake him up and send him home.

'Knock Knock'

I jump again and clear my throat so I don't sound as shaken up as I feel.

"C–Come in." The door creaks open and Darien's head pops in.

Stupid Adam couldn't even try to tell him to leave?

"Teleiótita? Come on we need to get going."

He looks good. I didn't think I could admit it to myself, but not seeing him for almost two weeks has left me… missing him and the chai tea he always brought me. I'd never say it to his face though. He'd probably laugh in my face if I ever said it. All the more reason to stay home. No one laughs at me from home.

"I–I'm not going." His face drops and I feel a little good about myself, but then I see it plain as day on his face.

He's not just upset he's hurt. It's weird to see such a open emotion on his face when he's always fighting himself. I hurt him and it hurts me. But I have to steel my heart and mind. He's getting inside, and that's not good because that's what Lydia wants. God, there's something oddly familiar about Lydia that I can't put my finger on. She wants to get in and break me. They all do. And he's proved to be no different from them.

"Teleiótita please come. I have everything planned out and I think you'll have fun and I just –I've missed hanging out with you. And I know what I did was wrong and it's ok to be jealous–"

"I wasn't jealous. It disappointed me. I thought… I thought you were different."

I thought I was a little special to you.

SPECIAL? HA! DON'T BE STUPID FREAK! THERE'S NOTHING SPECIAL ABOUT YOU! OH WAIT YES THERE IS… YOU'RE A SPECIAL CASE! A BASKET CASE! A DEFORMED FREAK OF A BASKET CASE! NO WONDER HE LEFT!

Lydia's voice echoes throughout my head and I shut my eyes closed to calm my breathing. Just because she's right doesn't mean I want to hear it right now. What I hear is the door swinging wide open and him walking towards me slowly. His footsteps stop in front of me and I take a peek at this gorgeous specimen of a sex loving jerk.

"I am different! Listen I get it you only said go have sex as a joke not seriously, but and I'm sorry but it's a part of me. A part of who I've become. Getting to know you has been amazing. Connecting with you… It terrifies and excites me. But old habits die hard. It's not an excuse but it is the truth."

There it is again. The open emotion on his face, honesty.

"Just come with me. We will have an awesome time. And if not… if not, you don't have to worry about seeing me." The idea has merit. If he finally leaves me alone, then the bullying will go back to a minimum. But… he's the only friend I've had in a long time. But he's not really my friend, is he?

"What would we be doing?" I ask meekly.

Darien reaches into his back pocket and pulls out an envelope. As he hands it to me I make note of the fact that his hand is shaking and there's a thumb print of sweat on the corner of the envelope. He's nervous. Maybe he will reveal the monster's plan today. That's the only reason he could be nervous. He will show his true colours… because he's a jerk. That hasn't changed about him. He's still a jerk and will always be one, and I can't let my guard down around him. I need to be strong.

Opening the envelope, all of that strength evaporates. I'm so weak.

"Di–Disneyland?" The tears well up in my eyes. He's such a jerk. I hate him. I hate him. I NEED to hate him.

"I remember you saying it's always been a dream of yours but you've never been able to because of the constant moving around. When you said I could–"

I run into his arms and hug him tighter than the fear of being hurt by him. I hold him and inwardly curse myself for being such a weakling and not putting up a better defense. I hate that I'm such a sucker.

"Do you like it teleiótita?" He smells so good and feels so warm and… *and holy crap! We've never hugged before!*

I pull back abruptly causing me to fall back onto my bed. My body is still tingling from his touch and I can feel the absence of his warmth. I shouldn't have done that. That was so stupid. Now he will want hugs all the time.

You think he wanted that hug? He was only being nice to you, you freak. He would want nothing more than a vomit bag from you.

She's cruel, but she's honest. She's so damn honest. And I need to be honest with myself. I need to stop giving in.

"You shouldn't have done this. You shouldn't be here. This makes no sense. You need to leave. I can–" He holds me in his arms and shuts me up.

I knew he would want hugs. I was just getting used to the hand touching. Oh God, why me? Why can't you cut me some slack? I may not believe in your works anymore, but I know you're out there. Please take me out of my misery!

"I told you it would be the best six hours of your life and I plan on sticking to my word. I just want you to trust me and not worry about everyone else around you."

"I don't have any sunglasses..." He hums and holds me closer.

"Why would you need them? It's not that sunny out."

"Isn't it obvious? To hide my face." He pulls back and smiles.

"I don't want you to. There's nothing to hide Arabella, believe me when I say that. You're beautiful and as much as you try to hide away it still shines as bright as ever." I bury my face back in his chest because his eyes are too intense. His everything is too intense. And I'm too weak.

"Stop saying those things to me, Darien. We aren't friends." I feel his chest vibrate with laughter. He's so warm.

"No we aren't friends are we? We're just us and I am more than happy to just be us again." I want to sleep on his chest. And maybe breathe it in and then bite it. I really want to bite him.

"We should get going then. You've already wasted thirty minutes of your six hours." I say reluctantly, pulling back. Again the vibration and he unwillingly lets me go. I hate him. Please God, let me hate him just a little.

"Definitely. I've already spoken with your brother, but I want to tell your parents first before we leave." My heart thuds at that.

They will think he's my boyfriend. They're going to over-react. They will want to take pictures. Oh brother.

"Ok." Darien smiles and I watch greedily as his eyes light up. His beautiful, normal green eyes. His beautiful green eyes on his overly attractive face. He's just too much.

He looks down at my hand and back up to me. There's no point in trying to be modest about this anymore. We've touched. We've passed boundaries I tried to set up. We've become… us.

"We've already hugged Darien you can take my hand with me flinching." But when he reaches for it, I still flinch. Weak girl. We walk down stairs, our hands still entwined and I watch for my family's reaction. They're blank for a few seconds before they smile.

"Have fun Arabella and keep warm." Mom says cuddling into my dad. He nods at Darien and smiles at me. No words from him.

"Be back before midnight. That's still our tradition, Ari." Adam says smirking.

"You hurt my sister. We hurt you. Straight forward." Alec says before he turns back to the T.V.

"See ya, Ella. And get me one of those turkey legs, will ya? There's a twenty on the counter." Adrian says as he stares into his phone. Alec and Adam perk up asking for one too and they give me extra money.

"You ready?" Darien asks, squeezing my hand.

I look back at my family acting so casual and then down to our hands. Why does it feel so weird?

Because you're a freak and you don't deserve nice things. You don't deserve the happiness Darien could give you. Let's be honest Arabella, he's only doing this for personal gain.

I frown and almost retreat back to my room, but Darien tugs me forward and out the door.

Thirteen

Six Hours

***D**arien*
    We arrive at the park and walk to the entrance. The entire time I watch Arabella. I need to make sure she enjoys this to the fullest and I will do whatever it takes to make sure she does. If that means pushing my darkness aside for the night I will. I can deal with the repercussionsussions of liking her later.

It doesn't take us too long to get inside and once we do I notice the park is very full. Not surprisingly it is New Year's Eve. I keep close to her and we maneuver our way to the center of the square so we can grab a map. I glance down at her and see a passive expression on her face.

I'm nervous. I'm so nervous I can't help my palms from sweating and my breathing won't slow down. And I know she can feel it. Our hands keep slipping so I try to keep our fingers interlocked. I'm practically panting and I can't control it. I just want today to be perfect. I want her to forgive me. I want her to want me the way I want her.

"I've got fast passes for the best rides that always have the longest rides and –"

"Where did you get the money to pay for all of this?"

"I had a job remember?" She nods and continues to take in her surroundings.

What she doesn't know about that job is that I left it after having sex with my manager. Remember the one that needed to get laid? Well, it seems she's the clingy type, and that's not my style. So I quit, took my money and moved on. I couldn't stand working there anyway.

"I have more than enough money for anything you want to eat or buy so go crazy all right?"

"I think you're crazy." She mutters while looking forward.

"I am crazy, but the good kind I've been told." She shakes her head, but I can see her smile.

I like it when I make her smile, it's different from all of her other smiles. She has her grimace/smile whenever someone insults her because she's trying to hide the pain she feels. She smiles wide and carefree with her brothers because they're her family and they love her unconditionally. She smiles lightly with Vincent because he's a friendly teacher who wants her to excel, but with me... it's different. It's my smile, it's the "You're an idiot Darien so leave me alone" smile and it's all mine.

"Why are you staring at me?"

"Why can't I?" Her face turns away from me and she frowns.

"Because when people stare they're looking at my deformity and no one stares at it in positivity. It's ugly, and it's rude." Arabella fluffs her hair so it covers her eyes more and looks down.

I can't stand it when she talks so badly about herself. I've met a lot of women that degrade themselves so others can compliment them, but it's not like that for Arabella. She really thinks she isn't beautiful. I don't know how many times I have to tell her she is gorgeous, but I'll never stop.

"Well I don't mean to be rude teleiótita but I stare at you because I get lost in your beauty and I end up losing track of everything around me. I'm surprised I can even walk straight." She giggles and bumps my side. My body is on fire.

"Shut up."

"Yes teleiótita." Arabella pauses and I turn to see her staring at me hard. Did I do something wrong? Did I say the wrong thing? She bumped me!

Isn't the bump a good thing?

"What's wrong?" She continues to stare before her face lights up and she runs at me.

"You promised you would tell me. So tell me." Am I crazy or is she crazy? Or is it the both of us?

"Huh?" She rolls her eyes.

"Tel-oshi-ta you said you would tell me what it meant today." I'm already blushing.

"Oh yes... ok well... it means perfection."

Her reaction is slow, but it gradually grows. Her nose wrinkles first and her eyebrows crease, causing her eyes to narrow and her lips to purse and then I'm thinking about her lips and about what they can do. But back to her reaction, she's just staring at me confused before my favourite blush dances across her skin.

She knows I watch it happen, and she lets me because deep down she likes it when I watch her. She likes that I'm turned on merely by her blushing. She likes the attention I give her even though she won't say it.

Her blush stretches down her chest and fans across the top of her breasts, leaving a deep pink shade in its wake. The blush isn't easy to see on her delicious brown skin, but I always find it either way. Man, her breasts are beautiful even if I haven't seen them and now I'm aroused. I can't focus.

"Perfection?" Her hand reaches up to her face, and she grazes her lips before looking back up at me. "You said that when we were in the classroom too... That's why you said it's something I know."

"Yes teleiótita means perfection because you are perfection to me. I find it much more endearing than baby or babe or crap like that." Her head shakes and she looks down as if she's ashamed of something.

"I'm not perfect. Look at me Darien. This is not perfect." I close the distance between us and take her in my arms... because I'm allowed to now... and it feels so good. I have to hold my hips back a little because I don't want her to feel how good this hug really is.

"I am looking at your Arabella. You may not be perfect to the world," I take her chin in my hand and raise her head to meet my eyes, "but you are perfect to me and I hope someday that counts for something."

Her lips purse again and her hand slides up my chest causing me to gasp out. I don't think she even realizes what she's doing right now. I want to kiss her so badly I can feel a buzz of energy on my lips.

"It counts." We both stare into each other's eyes and I think for a moment we're about to kiss. I lean my head down to hers and am a breath away from kissing her when she pulls back.

"Don't. Please." I smile warily. *I'm so turned on right now, it's the worst.*

"I'm sorry. I pushed it too far." She nods and looks away, holding herself.

I need to go slower with her. I need her to trust me again. I let my hand fall to my side and leave it hanging between us in case she wants to hold it.

"You have four hours and 50 minutes," she grabs my hand, "make it count."

***

Three hours left and we've been on *It's a Small World*, to which I wanted to tear their damn heads off, *The Haunted Mansion* and *Space Mountain*. The last ride was her favourite.

We took pictures with Mickey and Minnie mouse and we looked like a couple. I would say it to her, but I knew she'd get upset, so I kept it to myself. I bought an extra copy of the photo so I could keep it with me at all times.

Arabella wanted a snack, so I bought her a corndog nd we shared it. It's the second time we've shared food together. I purposely ate little bits so she would keep offering more to me. I'm a goner.

***

Two hours left, and we went back to *Space Mountain* before we rode *Indiana Jones* ride, the Pirates ride and the *Big Thunder Mountain Railroad*.

Arabella complained that she was getting thirsty, so I bought her a huge drink and two scoops of ice cream. She said she didn't want it but she ate it all anyway and said it was the best ice cream she's had in years. I was grinning like a fool.

***

One hour left, and we went rode *Snow White* before riding the *Alice in Wonderland* and some tea cups ride. I was dizzy for a few minutes and she held my hand the entire time. She led us to a bench where we sat together and enjoyed the scenery, and she told me stories about growing up in Texas for five years. She brought me water, pet my face and relaxed against me.

I pretended to be dizzy for ten more minutes after that.

***

"Are you sure you want to ride it again?" I ask as we are already halfway through Space Mountain.

"Are you chicken?"

Her happiness, it makes me want to jump off this mountain and fly. I did this… and not try to fly; make her happy like I've never seen before. Everything about her is glowing right now. Her hair even seems brighter, and it's so dark in here. She's smiled and laughed eighteen times today, all because of me. It builds me up when the memories try to tear me down.

"No I'm not a chicken I just didn't know you liked this ride so much." She turns back to me and smiles again before her eyes narrows and her eyebrow raises and now she looks sexier than sex.

"You know nothing, Darien Petros." Her accent sounds better than my own and I have to force myself not to kiss her because I want to… like really, really bad.

"You watch Game of Thrones?" Arabella shrugs her shoulders and runs the rest of the way to the ride, leaving me uncomfortably aroused again.

"Hurry Darien!" Her voice echoes from ahead and I follow it till I see her waiting in the line. "Took you long enough." Her hand grasps mine and I smile at her. I want to kiss her. Have I said I want to kiss her? The thought is driving me crazy.

"We have twenty minutes left teleiótita." She's leaning in to me right now. We look like a couple. We're not though, we're just us.

"Hmm."

"Don't forget about the turkey legs for your brothers."

"Hmm."

"Did you want a memento or something so you can remember these spectacular six hours?"

"Hmm." I look down at my teleiótita. She's got her eyes closed, a small smile on her face. She's so relaxed which is rare whenever she's in public. I wonder if it's just my doing or if she's realized that her eyes are beautiful not ugly. I squeeze her hand and she opens her eyes slowly.

"What is it?" The laughter comes bubbling out before I can stop it. She's so adorable.

"Did you hear anything I said?" She rolls her eyes and steps forward ruining our couple-looking moment.

"Yes you said we have twenty minutes left, don't forget about the turkey legs and if I wanted a memento." She looks at me pointedly and I smile back.

"Then why didn't you respond?"

"Because I was enjoying the moment you dope." My heart thuds and my palms get sweaty again. Just great, I will probably have a panic attack. I stare at her, at everything that is Arabella Seraphina-Rose Wilson, and sigh.

"Sorry I ruined it then." The line moves forward as she laughs to herself. I think I hear her say something about a puppy but I'm not sure.

We take a few more minutes before we're back on the ride again and this time; I choose to just watch Arabella; She screams and smiles and her eyes widen as we're blasted into the dark. Everything that makes her do what she does, I'm savoring it and tucking it in my mind for safe keeping.

The ride, Arabella's favourite ride, comes to a halt and we slowly trek back into the light and the awaiting staff to help us out. We get off and head to the main square to watch the parade.

The fireworks are amazing and the lights make Arabella sparkle. As she's watching the show, I take a few pictures of her reactions because she looks so peaceful right now and I want this side of her to last forever.

"Thank you for this Darien. I was apprehensive at first but... you- just thanks." She's barely able to peel her eyes away from the show to look at me, but I take the compliment all the same.

Looking at this beautiful woman, I realize that I don't want to lose this side of her. I never want to see her frown or degrade herself. I never want her to hide away from me or the world. I want her to be like this all the time and I want to be the one who can do this to her. I want to be everything and anything for her. I just want her.

Don't say it, Darien! Don't be an idiot and repeat your mistakes! SHUT YOUR

MOUTH–

"I love you Arabella."

She looks up at me with wide eyes and gasps. Her head shakes and her eyes well up in tears before she backs up, bumping into people along the way. I reach out to touch her and maybe take back what I said, but she turns around and runs away, three turkey legs flailing in the pocket of her backpack. She gets smaller and smaller until she is out of my sight.

I should have kept my mouth shut.

Fourteen

I'm So Lost

Arabella

It's time like these when I despise that Almighty being up in the clouds. He likes to torture me. I know he does because there's no other reason for what just happened.

No explanation.

No justification.

Nothing.

Either the Devil possesses Darien and is maniacally laughing at my idiotic reaction, or The Almighty planted him in my life to make me see a glimpse of happiness before taking it away. I mean… ok I know he wouldn't do that and really I have no one else to blame but myself but it is a theory.

DAMN IT!

I told myself not to give in. I built up walls and avoided everyone for a reason. And yet Darien was a leech. He wouldn't let go. He held on for dear life and he squeezed me so tight that I lost focus on what really mattered. And truly what really matters is… well… it's obvious… damn it I can't even remember anymore. That fool has tainted my mind and my morals. He whisked me up with pretty words and kind gestures and led me astray. I hate him… but he loves me.

I'm So Lost

"Arabella wait!" His voice is frantic yet distant. Foolishly, I run into a nearby store to catch my breath and hopefully throw Darien off my trail.

Looking back, I see Darien rushing straight towards me causing me to curse loudly alarming a little boy to my left.

"You shouldn't swear, lady." He says wagging his finger at me. I bite my lip.

"I'm so sorry! I didn't mean for that to come out." I say in a hurry. Darien has to be getting closer. I don't have time to apologize to a little boy. I need to get out of here.

"I hope to never hear that again, miss." He says picking up a pair of Mickey Mouse ears.

"I hope to never see you again." I mutter quietly.

I knew I shouldn't have stopped running. *Stupid girl. Stupid deformed girl*. I catch my breath before I continue to run through the square and straight to the exit. I don't even get to say goodbye to Goofy as I push past people.

Closing my eyes, I try to imagine that I'm home. That today never happened, even though it was one of the happiest days of my life. I imagine I am curled up on the couch with my family getting ready to watch the ball drop in New York. I imagine that this is all a dream, and I never met Darien Petros. But when smell his cologne to my right, I know I can't escape reality.

"Arabella... I know it must scare you... but I promise..." He stops and tries to catch his breath and I look at him panting with red cheeks and hair sticking up in every direction. He looks like a mess... *my mess*. But he can't be mine. He was never mine.

"Maybe it's too early for me to have said that... but I meant it. And you can ignore it and me but... it will always and forever be out there for you to know." He throws his head back and closes his eyes in exhaustion.

How can he love me? He doesn't even know me. I mean seriously. He can't love me. There's nothing to love. I am not loveable. No one would want to love me.

But Darien loves you. He just said it. Twice, technically.

Where's Lydia's snide voice now? Why can't I hear her? Have I grown so accustomed to it?

"Arabella?" My eyes travel back to him and my heart flutters at the sight of him all disheveled and nervous. That open pure emotion on his face. He's perfect right now and beautiful, so exquisite. I like the way vulnerability looks on him.

Darien hesitates to touch me, his hand slowly creeping towards my own. I watch his fingers flex as they get closer to mine before rests his hand on my own. Damn him. I don't like the way he fits perfectly with me. I don't like how comfortable I feel when he's around. I don't like how badly I wanted him to touch me again, that when he does I feel so good I want to lean into him and smell him… and maybe just maybe lick him because damn him if sweat doesn't make him look sexy.

"Darien you know nothing about me." He smiles lightly and walks a little closer to me.

"That's ok. We can get to know each other." I shake my head because even though Lydia isn't cackling, I can still feel it in my skin, feel it giving me goose bumps.

"No, that makes no sense." Again, he moves closer to me and I can feel the heat radiating off of him and it feels like home.

"It makes perfect sense teleiótita." Finally, we reach Darien's car. It's silent and I want him to go away and leave me alone, but then again I want him to stay near me and keep me warm. I'm so lost.

We reach the car easily, and he opens the door for me. I never realized before, but this is the first time I've been in his car. It smells just like him, with a hint of pine needles from the car freshener hanging from his rearview mirror.

The interior is neat and leather, which is stupid because sitting in leather in the summer must be hot. There's no garbage on the floor and no papers or CDs all over the place. It much more organized than I thought his car would be. It's odd because whenever he is with me, he seems to be such a mess; I just figured the rest of his life would be that way.

Darien places the Mickey Mouse plush doll and pictures on my lap and puts my backpack on the back seat. Closing the door, I watch him in the rearview mirror pace and talk to himself, ok no, he's arguing with himself, but then he sighs. I watch his shoulder slump forward and his body almost collapse on itself with exhaustion. I can understand why he feels that way... I'm exhausting to handle.

He runs both hands through his hair and walks to the driver's door. Getting in the car, he straps on the seat belt and turns on the car. And then he sighs, unclasps the seat belt and turns it off.

"Teleiótita... I love you. I know it's sudden and I know it makes no sense and I know I know nothing about you, but I love you anyway. I love your hair and how it smells like a rainforest. I love your skin and how soft and chocolatey it is. I love your lips and how plush they are." I turn my head away because he never sai–

"And your eyes. Oh my God, your eyes teleiótita. They are a gift from God blessed into a girl with such radiance. Eyes that sparkle when fireworks are reflecting in them. Eyes that are so true to who you are as a person, so beautiful that people can't help staring in astonishment because you're that gorgeous. Eyes that have given me a glimpse into your tormented soul and allowed me to see the sheer joy and light that is in you. Eyes that are so different and so similar. Eyes that I want to only be watching me. Eyes that widen whenever I compliment you, narrow when you're mad at me and roll when you know I'm acting like a goofball. Eyes that look at me with pure unadulterated desire even if you won't acknowledge it. Eyes that captivated me so much that I grew desperate to see them again. Eyes that I love with everything in me."

He stops to catch his breath and I feel my cheeks wet with tears. Darien turns to me and takes my hands in his.

"I know you must think how stupid it is for me to be in love with you after only two months. I know you must think there is nothing about you that can be loved. I know you're confused. But if you hear anything tonight, hear this, I love you so much that I won't ever allow you to get rid of me. You can push me away you can call me names and you can ignore me all you want, but I will always be here. And we can fight and argue and maybe even break up, but my love for you will only grow." I choke on a sob and gasp out.

"But why?" His soft fingers brush away my tears.

"Because you are you and we are just us and there's nothing else that I want more."

And just hearing him say those words, as vague as they are, it's enough. That is what I needed to hear. That is the light that cracked into my dark thoughts.

"Ok."

His smile never falters as he leans in and hugs me. And I don't feel ashamed to breathe in his scent and rub my face in his neck. I still feel stupid and I still feel deformed and I'm still so confused but it's ok for right now.

***

"So, do you guys do this every year?" Darien asks as we sit on the couch. He drove me home, and we barely spoke after his confession. Instead, we held hands and listened to the Yiruma CD he bought.

"Yup, we used to see it when we lived in New York. Our house was high enough to see it from our rooftop." Adrian says eating his turkey leg. Darien glances at me and puts a hand to his chest.

"You never told me you lived in New York teleiótita!" I roll my eyes and throw popcorn at his nose. He's so dramatic.

"It wasn't your business to know." He leans forward and smiles, his forehead almost touching mine.

"Touché." I pull back and knowing my entire family saw that. He doesn't seem the least bit nervous here. He's so relaxed and I'm trying not to seem like a jittery mess. Because even though we aren't together, we're still something and I know everyone can sense that.

"What do you do for New Year's Darien?" My mom asks as she walks into the kitchen. Something about his attitude changes. Now it almost darkens. It's something I've never seen before, but it's as clear as my eyes. He looks as though he is in pain as he frowns.

"Mourn."

His voice is barley a whisper, but I hear him. No one else does but I do. His eyes turn glossy and he closes them before taking a deep breath. Again, his demeanor changes and he smiles as if nothing happened.

"We celebrate. Nothing big, just my parents and I, but it's fun, regardless." He's lying. I never knew him to lie before. He's always so honest, not always his emotions but his words.

"Darien…" My voice is quiet to not draw attention. He turns to look at me with that fake smile still plastered on his face.

"Are you ok?" I ask slowly. He smiles even wider, and it's so big and so fake that I think his face might crack but he says nothing in response as he leans into me seeking comfort it seems. I rest my head on his shoulder and hold on to his hand. A few silent seconds pass before I feel him relax again.

"I'm great Arabella. I'm more than great." When he says that and looks at me, I know he's being genuine. Because he loves me and he's crazy and I'm crazy for thinking this will last but whatever for now.

"Ok." I say, pulling back.

He stares at me again like he did when we were at Disneyland. He stares at me with such obvious hunger I wonder why my family has said nothing about it yet. I mean even I can see his hunger… down there and he isn't even hiding it. Maybe he doesn't notice it yet.

I can see in his eyes he wants to kiss me. He wants it badly. Why in the hell he wants a kiss from me I don't know? There's nothing special about me. Nothing kissable about me. I know there isn't. Well, my lips are nice I can admit that but that's it.

When I share my first kiss, I want to be sure about it. I want to be sure that whoever I give it to deserves it… although…

Oh please, as if someone is dying for a kiss from such a frog? Get a grip freak. No one wants to kiss your botched lips.

I almost sigh at how twisted my mind is. I hate to admit it, but I missed that evil voice. That devil in my head. Little insufferable Lydia, always trying to bring me down. Constantly expressing what I truly feel and think. She is such a brutally honest girl.

"What's bothering you, teleiótita?" Darien asks touching my face. His fingers graze my lips, and something jolts through me and straight down to one of the ugliest parts of my body, the part that shall never be named.

"Nothing." I squeak out.

All three of my brothers turn to my voice. Simultaneously they watch Darien and my interaction through narrowed eyes. I smile awkwardly and turn away to face the T.V. There's about ten minutes left until the ball drop so we're just watching the performances so far.

"What was it like in New York?" Darien asks snacking on some popcorn with his free hand. I smile at him and shrug. I was born there, but I can't remember much since we moved when I was seven. Mainly the bad parts stay in memory.

"I can't say I remember a lot, but I remember Times Square being so bright and pretty and there were so many people around all the time. The streets were littered with bodies bumping into each other to get to their destination. I also remember it had the best pizza I've ever eaten. Like literally slices as big as my head for only three dollars and it was so cheesy and greasy and delicious." Adam laughs at that.

"Yeah, I remember Ari would always cry and beg mom to get pizza for lunch. You'd think she ate nothing else. I swear wasn't pizza like the first solid food she could eat dad?" My brother and my father laugh at that as he walks into the living room.

"My baby girl was a pizza freak. Still is I hope?" He looks at me and I smile wide.

"Dad!" Darien smiles as well and I fill him in. "My father and I always bonded over that pizza. We love pizza the most in this family and while everyone else will get annoyed, we never will." His hearty laugh makes me feel so happy inside. I love my dad. Mom finally joins us with cookies, cakes and hot drinks.

"Chai tea latte for Arabella and Adam. Green tea for Adrian. Orange pekoe for dad and me and two hot chocolates for Alec and Darien." She places the drinks down and we all thank her.

It's so odd. Everyone is acting so normal with Darien. No questions asked, and no eyebrows raised when we came home. They didn't tell him he wasn't welcome, instead they invited him to stay. There was no five feet apart rule for us, and Alec didn't threaten him once. Everything is just... odd.

"The countdown is beginning!" Mom says sitting down. Dad is in his lazy boy, so she sits on his lap.

"Ten! Nine! Eight! Seven! Six! Five! Four! Three! Two! One! Happy New

Year!" We can't jump up because of the drinks, so instead we all stomp our feet and blow our noise makers.

"Happy New Year teleiótita." Darien says as he leans close and nuzzles my nose. I blush and hide my face in his neck. He's such a jerk.

Fifteen

What a New Year

Darien

Once upon a time I would laugh at those who would talk about fate because fate ruined my life. But now... I can't say I'm happy about fate, but I have to thank it. Because of fate, I moved to Anaheim, California. Because of fate, I enrolled into college. Because of fate, I met Arabella Seraphina-Rose Wilson. Because of fate, I fell in love. For real this time.

"Stop staring at me like that." If it were possible, I'm sure there would be hearts in my eyes right now. Transparent hearts that only reflect images of Arabella.

"I always stare at you like this." I say nudging her side. She rolls her eyes and lets her hair fall forward. She's hiding again.

It's our first day back to school, and I felt like a god when I saw her eyes widen in surprise to see me in her driveway. She protested and said people would notice. I said I didn't want her taking the bus or relying on her mom if I could drive her. She said it was out of the way.

I laughed. And even though she hit my shoulder and said I was such a dork, she still hugged me good morning and took her chai tea latte. A couple people from my old calculus class smile and nod and I return it. People have been keeping a distance from us lately and I appreciate it, I don't want Arabella to feel overwhelmed.

I'm used to the attention I revel in it so I've never minded people crowding around me. It's different for Arabella. It's taken months for her to get accustomed to me. Besides, the people I've been associating with are the same ones that for some stupid reason don't like her. It's better this way.

"Yeah, but that was when we were alone. We're not alone now, so stop." She steps away from me. I know people are watching us. I know they must be curious why I'm still seeing "the freak" as Lydia put it. But I don't care what they think. They don't matter to me. Arabella does.

"I stare at you like this when we're with your family." She stops walking and sighs. The flashbacks have been getting worse the more I allow myself to feel. I have to drive them back more than before.

"Darien, I know you like to act like it but you're not stupid so please stop. No more following me around, no more staring. Just stop."

"Why should I hide how I feel for you?" I told her I loved her, and I didn't just say it for brownie points. I said it because I meant it and I wanted people to know it too because it's real and it's pure and she's mine.

We've been hugging so much lately. I love it. She likes it... she won't admit it, but she does. I can feel it when she takes in a deep breath of my cologne. One day she said she it smelled better than most cheap colognes guys wore so I bought three more and the shower gel to match it.

"Because I'm tormented enough!" I move closer to hold her, but she shakes her head and steps away.

"Please Darien." She wants me to back off as people bully her. She wants to take the pain all on herself and not let me help. She wants to be her own hero... and I have no choice but to let her. I can't get involved... I can't repeat my mistakes.

"Can we at least have lunch together?" She nods and walks away from me. As it's a new semester, we have new classes, so I head towards my Interpersonal skills lecture and groan when I see who's in it.

"Hi Darien!" Lydia's scratchy voice fills my ears and I cringe. I take a seat at the back of the hall and it's as if everyone else follows. I knew I was popular but this is ridiculous.

Taylor is in this class as well and when he walks in and sees me, he frowns. Who knows why he's upset? I really don't care. Either way, he still sits beside me.

"What's up, man? How was your break?" I ask, trying to be friendly. Truthfully, I'm not interested in hearing any of his stories, but I'm trying to be respectful.

"It was great. Not that you would know." My eyebrow rises at the attitude.

"What's that supposed to mean?" He shrugs and unpacks his notebook from his bag.

"It means you've been hanging out that weird looking black girl all semester and keep blowing me and the guys off. I mean, what the hell? Are you banging her or something? Is she that good?" My blood boils at his insinuation.

"If I want to spend time with Arabella, then I will. Not that it's any of your business." Everyone goes silent and I slump further in my chair, still feeling my anger build. Who the hell does he think he is talking to me like that?

"What crawled up his ass?" I hear someone whisper. My scowl deepens to where I'm sure I may never smile again in the class. This semester already sucks.

"It's that girl. She's like a witch or something, that's why she has two different colored eyes. She wears her hair wild like that to get more attention."

"I heard she gave him oral in an empty classroom on Halloween and she was so good he couldn't leave her."

"I heard since she's black she put some voodoo spell on him and he can't leave her side or he'll die."

"I heard she's actually just wearing contacts so she can get attention since her brothers are hot triplets and she's a nobody."

"Yeah, I bet those aren't even her real eyes. What a faker."

"How many times do I have to tell you she's a freak?" That was Lydia's voice. At her comment more people nasty talk about Arabella and that's when I see it. This disgusting look of smug satisfaction that she wears with pride. Why is she so evil? And why does she keep picking on Arabella?

No wonder why she's worried about having me by her side all the time.

This is what she's had to endure all semester. Enough is enough. I can feel the anger boiling like a kettle to where I can't take it anymore.

"WHY DON'T YOU ALL SHUT UP AND LEAVE HER ALONE! YOU'RE SUCH INSECURE PIGHEADED TWATS YOU WOULDN'T KNOW BEAUTY IF IT SLAPPED YOU IN THE FACE! DAMN IT!"

I throw my chair across the hall and it slams into a wall. Everyone is staring at me with open mouths and wide eyes. The teacher at the front gasps and turns bright red.

"Young man! Get out of my lecture right now! I am calling the Associate Dean!" I glare at her and everyone else. To think they treat Arabella with such blatant disrespect when she's done nothing to deserve it.

"Oh, I'll go if it means I can leave this room. I would rather be out of this hellhole than have to breathe the same air with such pompous, arrogant kids that have their noses stuck so far up their butts they can't smell the crap spewing from their mouths. Good riddance." I grab my stuff and storm out of the classroom.

And I almost thought I liked this school. What a joke.

Stomping my way all the way to the Associate Dean's office I drop my stuff on the floor. I don't care if I have an attitude. I don't care about anything except the fact that this school can allow such cruel acts to go unpunished. I mean I swear a few times and I'm sent to the Dean's office, but Arabella's bullied every day and no one does anything about it? Talk about a double standard.

"Darien Petros? The Associate Dean's office is just down the hall to your right. She will see you now." I look over to the secretary and grab my stuff.

Walking into the Dean's office, I am slightly surprised to see she is a woman. I mean I heard what the chick said but it never really sunk in. She motions to the chair in front of her desk and I sit down with a thump.

"You're new here. I met your parents last semester. Tell me Darien, why are you here? Your records show you seem to be a very troubled child." I roll my eyes, laughing.

"Records show only what certain people want you to see." Mrs. Matthews smirks and leans back in her chair.

"All right then Darien, what do you want me to see?" Looking down I clench my fists and sigh.

"I'm just a guy who's had it rough. So, I know what it's like to be hurting. What these students are doing should be inexcusable. To hurt such a precious girl who doesn't deserve-"

"So, your outburst is because of a girl?" I clamp down on my tongue. I shouldn't have said that! She will call down Arabella and then she will get mad at me for saying anything and our happy bubble will burst.

"Am I right?" *Think, Darien think!*

"Uh no! No! Not at all. I was um... just talking randomly." Mrs. Matthews smiles and shakes her head.

"If there's any bullying going on at my college, I want to know so I can put a stop to it. If you know of someone that is getting hurt in any way it is your duty as a friend to report it. No one should have to go through bullying alone." Sighing, I hang my head. She will hate me for this.

"Her name is... Arabella Wilson." She makes a tsk sound and pages the front desk.

"Send Arabella Wilson to my office, please." The minutes counting down till she gets here are excruciating. I can feel myself sweating bullets. She will kill me!

I can hear the moment she gets into the office. I don't know how I just know. The handle on the door turns and I feel my heart jump into my throat.

"You wanted to see me, Mrs. Matthews?" My god, it feels like I haven't heard that voice in years when really, it's been less than an hour. Her eyes fall on me before they turn impassive and she sits next to me. My hand automatically reaches out for hers because I want her to know I am here, and I can comfort her. But she doesn't take it.

"Arabella Wilson. We've spoken before." She nods and continues to look forward as if I'm not even beside her.

"From what Darien has told me, you have been struggling with offenders as of late." Her eyes cut to mine and I feel them slash through me.

"Is that what he said?" I gulp and sink into my chair. Mrs. Matthews watches us closely before she continues to speak.

"Arabella do you remember what I first told you?" I watch her sigh and see the tension release from her shoulders.

"I know but I can handle it." Mrs. Matthews smiles at Arabella softly.

"You shouldn't have to handle it on your own Arabella. And it seems Darien here thinks the same." Arabella doesn't look at me this time, but I can feel her frustration growing. She is so tired of me. *The cycle is repeating.*

"Do you know why he's here?"

"Because he's a snitch?" Arabella says under her breath. The laughter that fills the room is from Mrs. Matthews.

"No, because there were some students in the class that were talking about you, inappropriately and Darien retaliated. The choice in words he used and the actions he committed I do not condone, and he will pay his dues, but it was honorable." Her smile is sweet, and I smile back.

Arabella looks at me and then Mrs. Matthews and then shakes her head.

"I told you, Darien. I told you not to interfere." Again, I reach out to touch her and this time she literally recoils away from me.

"What did you expect me to do, teleiótita? They were saying demeaning things about you and about me and I wouldn't sit there and take it. Everyone here is so goddamn prissy and stuck up and they needed to hear the truth." She rolls her eyes, but when I attempt to touch her for the last time, she lets me.

"Now here's what will happen. Arabella, you will report to me whenever someone bullies you, this means; verbal or physical harm and I will deal with the responsible parties privately. If you want a teacher to talk to there are many within the school. Mr. Remington tells me you were his best and brightest student and we all would be sad if you lost that light." Arabella nods and squeezes my hand. Mrs. Matthews turns to me with a stern look crossing her face.

"Darien you are suspended for three days. I understand you were trying to defend someone you care about but damaging school property and endangering lives because you're angry will not be excusable. Please gather your belongings and leave the premises."

"Sounds fair enough." She nods and stands up.

"I will not be seeing you until Friday am I clear?" I clench my jaw but nod. "Yes ma'am."

"Good now both of you out of my office." She gestures to the door and we get moving.

Walking out hand in hand and I see Lydia, Taylor and two of the other people that were trashing Arabella sitting in the waiting area. Good, at least they're getting what they deserve. Lydia sees our entwined hands and scoffs before flipping her hair and looking away. Taylor bites his lip and nods as if understanding something. We try to leave but he gets in our way and I'm ready to deck him.

"Hey man, I don't want to fight. I just want to say I'm sorry. I didn't know. I hope we're cool." He looks at the two of us and then at our hands. I shrug and brush past him, bringing Arabella along behind me. When we get far enough, she pulls at my hand so we can stop walking.

"Arabella-"

"You got yourself suspended… for me." I turn to her and smile.

"Absolutely. I'd do it again if I had to." She giggles and runs a hand through her hair. It's curly than usual today, I wonder what she's done differently. Her eyes sparkle and I feel proud of myself.

"What did you say?" Smirking, I recall my appealing speech.

"Oh, I just called them twats that are too stuck up their butts to smell the crap spewing from their mouths." Her laughter bubbles up like a volcano and explodes. She's laughing so hard she snorts. It was once, and it was quick, but it was for me.

"Wow! I mean I've had so many comebacks in my head but that! That is just awesome Darien! Wow." When she catches her breath, a solemn look crosses over her face.

"Is there something wrong?" I don't know why, but it looks like she's battling with herself.

"It's just… you're suspended because of me. I don't want your parents to hate me. You shouldn't have done this, Darien. You shouldn't have gotten involved." I shake my head and reach out to hug her. She lets me, albeit reluctantly.

"Hey, I told you I'd do it again. We're us and no one can talk bad about us without some kind of repercussion. It's ok. My folks will be a little upset, but I've done worse."

"I don't want to be that girl…"

"You're not that girl teleiótita, you're my girl." She pulls back and narrows her eyes.

"We're not a couple Darien." Raising my hands in defense, I laugh.

"I know. I know. We're just us." I say smiling. Arabella's phone vibrates, and she checks the time before she looks at me sadly.

"Go to class. I'll be here when the day ends to drive you home." She bites her lip and people fill the hallways.

"Ok." She walks away and I hike my bag up on my shoulder and leave the school.

What a new year.

Sixteen

Days without Darien

Arabella

Like he promised Darien's outside waiting to pick me up. I hadn't seen Lydia or her alien hyenas all day and part of me feels relieved while the other part is on edge. It's rare that I'd go a day without some kind of torment and yet today there's nothing. It leaves me feeling a little unnerved.

"Hey teleiótita. How was the rest of school?" I shrug and get in the car.

I can hear his laughter from in here. He finds me being aloof funny. I think he secretly enjoys the chase. I'm not trying to make him chase me. I've told him to stop countless times.

Looking out the window I can see people's eyes watching us, curious, confused, and conflicted they all think what's happening is crazy. I don't blame them; I think so too, it's Darien who seems fine with everything.

"What's got you so down hmm?" He asks putting the car in reverse.

I didn't even realize Darien had gotten in the car, or maybe I did. My body seems to have instinctively moved closer to him and my hand is resting in the space between us, as if waiting for him to take it. Because he always does. He always takes my hand and holds it when he's driving. Even when I tell him it's a hazard that could get us killed, he doesn't listen. He never listens.

"Nothing."

What else am I supposed to say? How could I tell him that without the constant bullying it has left me feeling a little hollow and almost wanting? It's sick to say, but deep down in the twisted recesses of my mind I missed the teasing. I've become so accustomed to it that without it I don't know who I am. I know I'm crazy.

Yes, and crazy little freaks like you don't deserve Gods like Darien. He's a delicious sex God that will get bored with you like last time. He will find a gorgeous Goddess to thrive and ride on and he will leave you behind. Where you belong.

Little Lydia is feeling proud of herself today. She's happy with today's insults. She's happy because she knows it's true. We both know Darien is too good. I mean he's a mystery, and he's indifferent sometimes, but he's too good. He's way too good for me and he will go back to one of his flaky desperate girls and leave me in the dust. But it won't shock me when it happens. I'll be ready.

"I don't like the look that's crossing over you face teleiótita. Were those idiots bothering you again?"

He's holding my hand… how did I not feel it?

We're already halfway to my house… how did I not see it.

He's wearing more of his cologne… how did I not smell it?

How long have I been spacing out?

"No one was bothering me. Not a single person…"

"That's good, right?" I can hear it. He wants the praise. He wants to know that what he did was good and that I am happy he did it. I'm not happy though. If anything, he's made things worse.

But…

"Yeah it is. It's different, but it's good. Thanks again." His face lights up and I watch his face like there weirdo I am and lap up his happiness because his happiness is so damn contagious and it's a light that I haven't seen in so many years.

"Will you smile for me, teleiótita? I haven't seen you in hours and I've missed your smile." I roll my eyes and bite the inside of my cheek. I'm not smiling because he asked me to. There's nothing to smile about today. Nothing at all.

"I'm not in the mood to smile." In the corner of my eye I can see his face fall. Why is he so damn annoying?

"You'd smile if I were your brothers." He didn't mean for me to hear it, but I did. I don't feel guilty and I don't feel bad. I can't please everyone and I'm not trying to. He will make the next three days at school hell and that doesn't make me want to smile.

No, in fact it makes me want to scream.

***

Day One

He drove me to school this afternoon, and he bought me my chai tea. We were both hesitant on the goodbye because we've never had to part ways so quickly before. He usually walks me to class and lingers around until the last minute and he has to run to his class. We would argue about him being so stupid to jeopardize his attendance for someone that doesn't want him to be hanging around in the first place and he would always laugh and play with my hand.

But now it's different. Sitting in his car I can feel like there's some kind of invisible thread that is hanging between us and when I get out of this car, it will snap. I don't want it to snap… or maybe I do.

This is it, freak! He will tell you to get out so he can run off to some girl's house… maybe even to my house to do the nasty! He's got three days free of you to do whatever the hell he wants! And he will! Because he can!

Lydia could be right… no, she's most likely ninety-five percent right. What else is he going to do? I mean, he's like addicted to sex or something like that. He can't keep waiting around for me because I sure as hell won't be giving it to him. I'm not giving him a damn thing!

"Teleiótita? Are you ok?" He touches my hand and my head snaps in his direction.

He's a sex freak! He's a man whore! He wants so much sex! And not from you! No one wants a freak!

Her voice is clucking in my mind like crazy! Maybe I am crazy! And he's crazy for sex! He can't be trusted!

"Arabella!" Darien holds my face in his hands and shakes me a little. Lydia's voice dies down and I catch my breath.

"I'm fine." Pulling away, I take my stuff and leave his car. He's a man whore. What more can I expect then for him to live up to the name?

***

Day Two.

School was eerily quiet. No one made any rude comments, so I cowered away into my thoughts to get my daily beating. These students may not have been speaking out loud, but I could read their faces and that was loud enough. The teachers were overly nice, and I saw no sign of Lydia and her alien hyenas. At lunch I was on edge and needed something normal. Vince.

"Hey, Arabella, right on time." His door is open, and his classroom is normal and he's normal and I can breathe again.

"Mr. Remington, have you noticed people have been acting weird lately?" He laughs and pulls out his lunch.

"Valerie, or as you know her Mrs. Matthews, warned everyone about the dangers of bullying. She said if she hears any more reports about bullying at her school that that person will be charged and expelled. I guess it spooked the kids. She even brought cops on the premises for extra flare." What can I say to that? What is there to say? She said she would handle it and I'm grateful she did, but it won't last. It can't last… can it?

"Oh." Vince looks at me expectantly and then shakes his head.

My mind is always on all things "Man Whore". I'm embarrassed to think he can have such control over my thoughts after such a brief time of knowing each other.

"Yeah, I remember hearing about that." Yiruma plays filling the silence and I eat my lunch with nothing more to say.

The rest of the day is a blur. Without Darien, I slink through class. Nothing is of importance and nothing stands out. There are no mean words said, but they're written on faces and in body language and that's more than enough.

People don't always have to speak to express what they're feeling. I have eyes and I can see. I can see what they're thinking because they don't care to hide their disgusted expressions. I just use the darkness in my mind to fill in those stares with words and boy is their vocabulary harsh.

And yes, it's only in my mind and no, they aren't saying it out loud, but I know what they're saying. I've always known what they were saying. I can hear it louder than their laughter filled voices as I leave this hellhole.

"Teleiótita!" He's right where he was yesterday, but he looks like a completely different person.

I stop mid-stride and examine this infuriating boy. His hair is all over the place, his pupils dilated and his face flushed. His pants have an odd stain on them, his socks aren't matching and his shirt is messy. It looks a little dirty like he picked it up off the floor. He's wearing a light jacket, but it can't hide the red lipstick stain on his shirt. Why am I not surprised?

Taking out my phone, I dial Adam's number and he picks up on the second ring.

"What's up Ari?" I look away from Darien and walk back up the steps to school.

"Can you pick me up?"

"Why? Isn't lover boy driving you?" I sigh. My brothers have taken a liking to that nickname. Darien doesn't seem to mind, but I do. That name… it insinuates things… Things that aren't happening between us… Things that may never happen. I jump when I hear Darien's steps coming closer and end the conversation quickly.

"Just come and get me, Adam." I hang up just as Darien turns me around.

"Teleiótita did you not see me?" His hand is still on my shoulder and we both watch in silence as he slides it down my arm and into my hand. Such deafening silence.

"Oh, I saw you Darien. I'm sure everyone can see you. Loud and clear." I try to pull my hand from his, but he won't let me. Up close I can't see any hickies or bite marks like the last time he went back to his disgusting ways, but his clothes say enough. The words are screaming at me with the guise of Lydia's voice.

SEX! SEX! SEX! SO MUCH SEX HE ALMOST FORGOT TO PICK YOU UP! SO MUCH SEX WITH SEXY PEOPLE HE'S STILL DISORIENTED! SEX! SEX! SEX! AND NONE FOR YOU!

I shake my head and try to ignore the obvious truth. Though why ignore it when it's clear as the sun shining down on us. Something like a punch hits me in the gut and I look around for the offender but find no one. My stomach still hurts, and Darien won't let go and it's all too much.

It should take Adam ten minutes to get here, so I'll just go to the library and hide myself away like I'm supposed to. Again I try to pull my hand free, but Darien won't let go.

"Where are you going, teleiótita? My car is this way."

"I'm not going anywhere with you." His grip tightens and then releases.

"What did I do this time? I wasn't even here."

"Isn't that the point?" He looks lost. He's such a puppy. He's a man whore, sex loving, jerk of a puppy.

"Arabella," he only says my name when he's serious about something, "I can already see what you're thinking and no I did not have sex. I woke up late and rushed to get to you on time. I didn't want you to think I forgot about you." He's stroking my arm. He's never stroked my arm before. It feels good. He feels good. He's too good.

"What about your shirt?" There's no point in beating around the bush. I'm tired, frustrated and tormented by the ugly stares of everyone around us. I just want to go home.

"I searched through my dirty pile. It's a shirt I wore to a party a few weeks ago. I'm kinda lazy with laundry." He's blushing and scratching the back of his neck. He's embarrassed… he's telling me the truth. People are watching even more. We've created a scene. Lydia will eat me alive.

"Ok." He smiles wide and hugs me, but I push him back and frown.

"If that's a dirty shirt, I don't want it touching me." His laugh, his beautiful annoying laugh fills my ears and for a second, I can't hear the evil words. It's only a second, but all I can hear is his glorious laugh.

"All right fair enough. But you have to agree to at least holding my hand. I haven't seen you all day. I feel deprived." I nod, take his hand and we walk to the car together. I send a quick text to Adam as Darien drives.

Arabella: No need to come. Be home soon. He responds immediately.
Adam: Figured. C ya.

I roll my eyes. What is there to figure?

***

Day Three.

They allow Darien to come back tomorrow. I will never tell him, but... I've missed him. So much... too much.

***

"Ugh, I was enjoying my time away from school." We aren't touching, at my request, but he's leaning into me. He does that to ward off the guys. That's what he says at least. But I know no one wants me. Except Darien.

"Well suck it up. You're here now." *And I've missed you.* The thought is bad. I shouldn't think like this.

He smiles down at me; he must be around six feet, which is damn tall compared to my five foot three. Maybe I should wear heels around him that way I won't seem so small. Wedges are much easier to walk in than high heels. I wonder if he'd like them... But that's only if he stays with me. Attached to me.

He really is a puppy following around his master, always looking for her approval. He always wants to stay by her side because there's nothing holding him here but himself. He can leave whenever he wants... and I would let him.

"I will admit I've missed you, teleiótita. I mean driving you around is great, and I appreciate your parents not kicking me out every time I ask to stay over after school but when we're not together it's... weird. I always miss you. I'm addicted to you."

I shake my head and stand outside our lecture hall. We only have two classes today and apparently, they're together, so basically we have the entire day together. It's obvious he could weasel his way with the administration to adjust his timetable. What a creep.

"That's stupid. People shouldn't like rejection." He smiles and I hate his smile because I feel my stomach wobble at the sight of it.

"But you haven't rejected me in a month, so I'm hooked." He's right. I've been getting lenient. I've become too used to him. I'm getting attached to Darien. This isn't good. This can't be good.

"Hey Arabella?" I nod my head, but I'm not listening to him because I'm thinking about the consequences of this unknown happiness. The happiness my family gives me differs from this. I don't feel warm and fuzzy when my parents compliment me. I don't get woozy from the smell of them. I don't want to lick them either…

Uh Oh. Little Freak has got it bad, doesn't she? You want Darien like the pathetic clingy desperate freak you are. Let's see where this will go. I can't wait for it to blow up in your face. It always does and it always will.

The darkness clouds my mind again. The nasty words are screaming out. Little Lydia is sharpening her hot pink pitchfork and applying another coat of lip gloss. I can hear the smack of her lips and the cackles resounding throughout my mind. Her words are ringing like a bell.

You're a freak!

You don't deserve happiness!

Darien is only using you!

He doesn't love you!

It's all a trick! And you're falling for it!

"Can I call you Belle? It's not that I don't love to say your name because I do, but I like how Belle sounds. But if you don't want me to, I won't-"

"What?" Darien grimaces and runs a hand through his hair. He was talking all this time?

"Sorry I knew it was stupid to ask. I was just hoping because your family all have their own nicknames for you and I-" He's only talking about a nickname. No worries. No need to freak out. Just calm down, Arabella. Breathe.

"It's fine. The name is fine. I should go." I try to leave, but he traps me against a locker and smiles down at me.

"You know Belle means beauty, right?" Damn him I can't stop the twitching of my lips.

"Yes I know what it means Darien. Now shouldn't you be leaving?" His eyes are sparkling. Why is he so excited? It's just a damn name. Almighty, help me out here! This boy is crazy.

"Have you forgotten that we have class together?" He smiles again and leans towards me once more.

I completely forgot.

He wants to kiss me. He's been doing this a lot. He'll lean down to my face and stop just inches from my lips. He's a tease and I can't stand him. But I can't resist leaning towards him. He's always smelling so good and being so nice and smiling so brightly and loving me too much. He's making me want this kiss as badly as he does and damn it, it's working.

His lips are a mere breath away that I can taste the mint gum on his breath. I can feel the electricity sparking between us. He's so close. But not close enough.

"You're a jerk get away from me." I say pulling back. He's like a fridge and I'm that picture magnet that no one really likes but has to put it up. From time to time people will knock me off that incessant, strong, good smelling fridge but no matter what I still come back to it, holding on. Stuck to that damn fridge. Magnetized to it.

"Sorry sometimes I can't help myself." His eyes are wide again, and his breath is coming out in pants. He's so dramatic.

I look down and let my afro fall forward. People are watching again. I can feel their stares burning my skin. We're causing a scene and he doesn't care. But why would he? Everyone loves him and he loves- whoa! Just whoa! My eyes skim the waistband of his jeans and just... wow. When did his little neighbor wake up? And why does it look so... not little?

"I've noticed." I say pointedly. I don't have to look up to know he's probably blushing. His hand goes through my hair to push it out of my face, lifting my head up and brushing the side of my cheek. I've always hated when people would touch my hair, but Darien is not people. To my surprise, he's not blushing. No, this moron is smiling. Like a full-blown alpha male smile.

"I want to see your eyes before class." *And I want to keep them away from you. I don't want that intensity. It's too much to handle. You're too much. Every inch of you is too much.*

He grips my chin softly and raises my head. "Open your eyes, Belle." I don't even realize my eyes are closed. But when I open them, green comes into focus. Flecks of gold around the pupil that's widening as I draw closer to him. He's so... he's just so-

"Beautiful." I gasp and pull back. What did I just say? He seems shocked too. Why am I losing control? I need to be stronger. I need to be harder. I try not to peak back up at him but when I do, I see a look of pure raw hunger that makes me rush into class.

But where the hell am I supposed to hide if we have class together? Too bad this class doesn't last forever because like I said people don't have to speak to express what their feeling and in Darien's eyes, I know what he wants. And I'm not strong enough to run away.

Seventeen

Can I Kiss You Again?

Darien
I heard what she said. I felt it in my body and in my heart. I can still feel it now. It's a deep craving that's crawling up my spine and creeping into my very being. The old me is peaking his stupid head again. He's pushing back my barriers and resurrecting old desires. He's trying to take control.

She's never openly complimented me before and like the pathetic sap I am, I'm lapping it up and bathing in it. Because she thinks I'm beautiful and even though most men would prefer to be handsome, I am beautiful. The throbbing below was just a byproduct of her acceptance of my new nickname but now, I wince at the pounding its giving me… the hunger I'm feeling.

"Hey Darien wait up." I can't stop; my body isn't in my control. Or maybe it is. Because I am just now noticing how fast I'm walking. I didn't even notice I left our lecture hall but if I slow down, then I will turn around, tear Arabella from that hall and maul her like the animal I am. I want her so badly my head is hammering.

"Darien. Dude!" Taylor's on my left and who knows where Matt is. Better yet, who cares?

"Hey." I'm still a little pissed at him for what he said. For even uttering those disgusting words in my presence and about the girl I love no less.

"Listen I hope we're still cool. I won't say anything about your girl anymore. It wasn't right of me to do that." I nod and follow him to his elective class. He apologized before and I've been told she wasn't bothered since. No point in dwelling on it any further. Besides, Taylor is much more tolerable than Matt.

"Yeah whatever." He smiles and I realize he wants this friendship to continue. I don't know what the enormous deal is. In a few months we'll all graduate and continue further to get degrees in big universities and probably never speak again. No point in trying to push something that won't last.

"So, I heard you're suspended." Smirking, I sit at the back of the class and drop my bag.

"Yeah, I was using inappropriate language. Doesn't help what happened with the chair either." Taylor laughs and sits beside me.

"If it wasn't directed at me, I would have been laughing at the look of everyone's faces. Even the teacher looked like she wanted to crap herself. Remind me to never get you mad again." Shaking my head, I lean back in my chair and watch the clock.

Just two hours until I'm with Arabella again. We have all day together and I don't know what I will do when I see her again. I altered my timetable to match hers. Yeah, it's a little weird, but I wanted to make sure no one picked on her when I wasn't around. She may take it, but I would not let her anymore. She shouldn't have to endure such pain all the time. She's too pure for that.

"Well, sometimes people need reminding not to mess with the girl I care about." The statement comes out bitter and leaves me a little angry.

This must be how her brothers felt when she was a kid. I have this powerful urge to find everyone that ever hurt her and beat the crap out of them just to show them she has someone in her corner. Taylor nods, knowing my anger isn't about at him.

"True. If I had a girlfriend-"

"We're not dating." He looks at me confused but shrugs, regardless.

"Well whatever. If I *cared* about someone that much and people were saying rude stuff about her, I'd retaliate too."

"Glad you understand."

"Of course man." The teacher stands up from her desk and begins her lesson.

"Hey." Taylor pokes my side and points to his phone.

Taylor: I need a favor.

Darien: What's up?

I watch from my peripheral as Taylor takes a deep breath and types again. Something is bothering him.

Taylor: You remember that girl from that party we went to the beginning of the year?

Is he serious right now?

Darien: No.

Taylor: Right sorry. The girl who had the bright red hair at one party, then she had the pink hair and now her hair is like dark blue? She was grinding on the couch and gave me a lap dance?

I vaguely remember a girl with many hair colors.

Darien: Kind of why?

Taylor: So, I like her, right? But I don't know what the hell to say to her. Do you mind just... you know talking me up?

Darien: What are we in middle school?

Taylor: Come on man please! I like this girl, but every time I talk to her I end up sounding like an idiot.

Darien: Ok but if I talk you up what's stopping you from sounding like an idiot again?

Taylor: CONFIDENCE??

Taylor: PLEASE

Taylor: PLEASE

Taylor: PLEASE

Taylor: PLEASE

Taylor: PLEASE

Taylor: PLEASE

Taylor: PLEASE

I have to turn off the vibration on my phone because it won't stop buzzing. I look over to Taylor and the guy looks desperate. Sighing, I shake my head and reply.

Darien: What's her name?

"Yes!" The class looks back to me and Taylor and laughs. The idiot turns bright red and sinks in his seat.

"Is there something exciting about Euthanasia Taylor?" The teacher asks, annoyed. He shakes his head and sinks even further.

"No ma'am. Sorry."

"That's what I thought." She turns back to the board and Taylor goes back to text.

Taylor: Her name's Chelsey Hammond and she's majoring in graphic design. She has a spare next period she spends studying most of the time. She usually hangs out in the library in the fiction section reading or she would volunteer with the librarian.

I stare at the text in disbelief. I thought I was crazy about Arabella and yet Taylor makes me look normal.

Darien: all right. I'll text you when I'm done.

Taylor: Thanks so much, man.

Darien: Yeah.

I spend the rest of class going through my pictures of Arabella. They range from Disneyland, to her house, to her falling asleep in my car. By the time I've gone through them a fourth time, Taylor's class is over.

Eagerly, I text Arabella. I want to see her and touch her and smell her and eventually kiss her. And then I'll keep kissing her and make her crave my touch like I do hers.

And then finally… sex. Lots and lots of sex. I need to take a breath… Man, my imagination is way too vivid. I'm getting ahead of myself. And getting over excited. Again.

Darien: Meet me in the library in 20

Teleiótita: Why?

Darien: I thought you'd like a little down time somewhere quiet. Besides, we have two hours till our next class.

Teleiótita: Yes but the library?
Darien: I thought you loved the library?
Teleiótita: I do… when no one is there to bother me.
Darien: I thought we established I'm not a bother anymore
Teleiótita: I think you think too much.
Darien: You keep me on my toes.
Teleiótita: What was the point of this conversation?
Darien: Meet me at the library.
Teleiótita: What's the catch?
Darien: No catch, just meet me in 20
Teleiótita: We'll see if I show.

I love when she plays hard to get. When girls are too easy, there's no fun in the accomplishment of gaining their affection. I've been around gullible girls all my life. And sure the sex is great and even sometimes fantastic… but it still leaves me hollow and ultimately alone.

Coming to this school I tried to change, but I fell back into my old ways because it's so much easier to do… Thankfully Arabella is the change that I needed.

I head straight to the library and get a text from Taylor. It's a picture of this Chelsey girl and she's cute. Arabella is much better looking, but this girl is cute.

I spot her in the fiction section like Taylor said and put on my most charming smile.

"Hey you're Chelsey, right?" She looks up from her book and smiles at me.

"Yeah. And you're Darien Petros." I take a seat in front of her and wink.

"You know who I am?" She giggles and puts her hair behind her ear.

"I'd be stupid not to." She's flirting with me. It's obvious to see. I'm not even the least bit interested.

"Well, I've heard about you Chelsey." She blinks a few times and blushes.

"I'm guessing it's the parties last semester? It was my first time drinking, and I went overboard."

"Oh, that's no big deal. Trust me, I've done much worse." She perks up at my comment.

"Really?"

"Yup. I remember when I first moved here, I was just getting used to the atmosphere and there was this beach party. I got drunk and wandered towards to the shore. The under current dragged me in, and I was too tipsy to swim." Her face is showing horror.

"Everything was getting dark and I remember thinking to myself, 'I can't believe I never got to go to Disneyland'." She giggles and leans closer to me.

"Anyway I just remember someone grabs onto my arm and pulls me back to the shore." Chelsey's eyes widen.

"Who was it?" I grin because I know after this, she will be hanging off every word my Taylor will say.

"Taylor Montgomery." Her head pulls backs and her eyes narrow.

"Really?"

"Yup. That was how we became friends. He saved my life." The look on her face shows she doesn't believe me.

The truth is, I got plastered on purpose. Something triggered me that night and I decided that maybe.. maybe it would be best if I... if I didn't exist anymore. I wanted to die. I'd been at peace with the thought but Taylor saved me anyway.

"He doesn't seem like the–"

"Heroic type? Yeah, he can be an idiot and annoying but the man's got heart. And he's fiercely protective of the ones he cares about. Most of the time he acts like he's a jerk,, but he's not a terrible guy once you get to know him." Her eyebrows raise and she looks away, biting her lip.

"Really?"

"Really, really." She smiles and I mirror it.

"Well then, what about you?" I hear some movement behind me and lean closer.

"What about me?" She licks her lips and bats her eyelashes.

"What's your type?"

"Why do you want to know?"

"I've heard a lot about you, Darien Petros. I've heard rumors of your exciting encounters and your adventurous tastes. I've heard you've been so good that sometimes they orgasm at the memory of you." I nod and smirk.

That's no surprise. Girls can't keep their mouth closed about what I can do. It's a gift.

"And what about it?"

"Are you still available? For anything?" She asks coyly. Her body language seems more than inviting, but there's something about the way she's looking at me that throws me off. Regardless, I'm not taking the bait.

Arabella and I may not be a couple, but I sure as hell won't be making that mistake again. Besides, my hand can work wonders in the shower and like I said my imagination goes wild for Arabella.

"Depends on who's asking." I ask, just playing along. If this girl is a slut, then there's no way she should be with Taylor. He deserves better than that.

"I am." She answers back with no hesitation.

Wow. I mean I knew she was flirting, and it was fine because I'm not falling for it or her, but I am trying to talk up my friend and she's ready to jump my bones.

"Sorry I'm taken." The disappointment is obvious on her face. But then she smiles again.

"Good.".

"Huh?"

"It's obvious that you're trying to make Taylor look good to me so I was just testing to see if you were one of those sleazy guy friends willing to sleep around even if it hurts a friend." I laugh because what else am I to do.

"Wow. I underestimated you." She smiles and gathers her stuff.

"Well, what would you know about me other than that I am a magnificent dancer and a lightweight drinker?"

She winks and leaves me sitting there. I like that girl. She'll be good for Taylor. I text him everything I told her and he responds with a big smiling face and a thank you. He's not a terrible guy at all.

Getting up, I glance around the library to see if Arabella has shown up yet. I went over the time limit I set for myself, but it's still within the twenty-minute mark. I check every inch of this place and I clue in that she's not here. I would have figured she would come and she would frown and roll her eyes at me. She's keeping up this playing hard to get act.

Darien: It's been twenty-six minutes teleiótita. Where are you?

I wait for a response, but she doesn't reply. That's odd.

Darien: If you really don't like the library that much we can go outside?

Still no response. I wait a few minutes before I text her again.

Darien: all right, I give. We will go wherever you want.

After another twenty minutes of no response and I'm getting worried.

Darien: Teleiótita is everything ok?

Darien: because if I did something wrong I will apologize right now.

Darien: I did something, didn't I?

Darien: Ok teleiótita whatever I did please just tell me.

Darien: I'm covering all bases and apologizing right now. I AM SORRY!

Darien: Arabella?

I wait in the library until five minutes before our next class and leave. Maybe something happened to her phone. Yeah, that makes sense. She smashed it the first time we met, anyway. It could definitely happen again.

Walking in I see her seated near the back and I smile at the empty seat beside her. What makes me stop in my tracks though is when Chelsey sits beside her. She's in this class? I put on a smile and scan Arabella's face for any traces of anger instead of her usual annoyed look.

"Teleiótita you didn't answer my messages. Is everything ok?" She doesn't even look up. She's doesn't even flinch! What the hell did I do now?

"Take a seat class and let's get started." The class tries to conceal their groans, but I hear them anyway. I sit behind Arabella and stare at the back of her head, trying and failing to make her look at me. What did I do now?

Chelsey looks back at me smiling, and Arabella catches it staring at her. What is it now? I feel like a child getting scolded for something I never did.

"All right class I will pair you up for the semester's final assignment. You will need all the time you can get to work on this efficiently." The teacher lists off some names and I continue to watch Arabella fume.

"Darien and Chelsey. Arabella and Austin. Tyler and…" We're not paired together? Why aren't we paired together? I'm about to raise my hand to object when the teacher scans the crowd and shakes her head.

"And no, you cannot switch partners. The most I can allow is to group together in groups of four, but only that. These will be your partners for the rest of the semester. Now you can spend the rest of this class going over the assignment and dividing up the work however you want. Make sure you have a basis for your idea so you can explain it to me by the end of class. I must approve your idea before you continue to work."

This Austin kid, one I've never seen before, walks over to my teleiótita and plops down beside her with an ugly smirk on his stupid face. He's lanky with shaggy blonde hair and brown eyes. He's typical and Arabella is too unique for typical guys.

"Hey, I'm Austin." She doesn't look at him when he speaks. Good. She should only look at me. Because I matter to her and he doesn't.

"Arabella." She responds into her notebook. He leans closer to her and I'm two seconds away from choking this kid.

"Yeah, I heard. It's a beautiful name." Ha! The idiot! She hates it when guys pull cheesy crap like that!

"Thanks. Did you want to organize the work or–" Why didn't she get mad or annoyed or something?

"Sure, just tell me what you're good at and I will tell you what I can do and we can go from there." She nods and reads the assignment. He's leaning closer to her. I want to kill him.

"Hey Darien, what a coincidence." I barely even glance at Chelsey as Arabella continues to read. Who does this kid think he is? Why is he so goddamn close to my teleiótita? Does he want to die?

"Darien?" Someone touches my arm and I growl at them. Chelsey looks at me and then in the direction I'm staring before giggling.

"I'm guessing she's the girl you're taken with? She's nice, actually. She's helped me a lot last year." I grunt and continue to brood. Why is she being so nice to him? She wasn't even remotely nice with me when we first met!

"She's pretty. I've heard she has two different colored contacts. I wouldn't really know since she never looks me in the eye when we talk."

"They're not contacts. They're her real eyes. She has heterochromia." I say in annoyance. Chelsey nods and smiles even wider.

"Hey Ms. Fonseca said we can group together, right?" Again, I grunt.

"Your point?" Chelsey rolls her eyes and gets up. She walks to Arabella and Austin and pulls her chair behind her.

"Hey Arabella. You mind if we join your group? I think it will be easier to decipher all of this together, don't you?" My god! Chelsey is a genius! Austin smiles at her and moves over while Arabella continues to glare.

"Come on Darien, we don't have all day." I look at Chelsey, I mean really look at her and I realize she is pretty.

With a light shade of brown skin, not as smooth and gorgeous as Arabella's, and dark brown eyes. Her hair is big and very curly and the tips of it are blue, matching her shirt. Her cheeks are a little big making her smile that much brighter and she's an average height. Taylor is a lucky guy.

But as I get up suddenly, I'm unsure about going to Arabella. She's mad at me for sure, and it seems directed at Chelsey a little too. I don't know what I did, but I don't want her to be mad. I just want her annoyed. At least I know how to work with annoyed.

I pick up my chair and book and sit next to the empty spot beside Arabella. Slowly I reach out to touch her arm and she doesn't flinch away, but I can feel how tense she is. She's like a volcano that's waiting to erupt.

"Sup? I'm Austin." Chelsey smiles.

"I'm Chelsey. I'm majoring in graphic design." Austin smiles at that and nods.

"Sounds cool! Why are you taking academic writing then?" He says grinning at her.

"I love to write. So, I weaseled my way in here. Had to charm the administration. It was fun." Chelsey says pulling her hair into a ponytail. Arabella scoffs.

"Or slutty." We all look at her, and she continues to stare down. She's never been this outspoken before.

"Um." Chelsey narrows her eyes.

"Let's just brainstorming ideas." I blurt. Everyone nods and opens their books. Class goes by slowly with me touching Arabella occasionally, and her still being tense and muttering things under her breath. By the time class is over, she storms all the way to Vince's class.

"Teleiótita can we talk now?" She turns on me and grits her teeth.

"Why did you ask me to come to the library?" This catches me off guard.

"Because I wanted us to spend time together."

"Oh? It wasn't because you wanted me to hear that you're still in the game?" What the hell does that mean?

"What are you talking about?" She rolls her eyes and clenches her fists.

"I can't stand you; you know that. I never wanted you to bother me. I never wanted your attention or your affection and especially not your love. I just wanted to be left alone. I didn't want to feel these things. I didn't want it." My breathing stops and I feel my heart race.

"I couldn't help falling in love with you Belle and I don't regret it. I'm sorry if it's a lot to handle and I'm sorry if it can annoy you to have me around sometimes, but I love you." Shaking her head, she kisses her teeth.

"I heard everything you said in the library to Chelsey today. I heard it all, and I knew that this day would come. I knew that you would finally show your true colors. I just didn't think you would be so cruel about it."

"What are you talking about?" I repeat. I can tell when her nose wrinkles like that she's about to blow.

"You wanted me to hear that you would hook up with her! I heard everything about your adventurous tastes and orgasmic stories! I heard it all! I heard you indulge that little slut's fantasies and I know you wanted to have sex with her, you pig-headed, disgusting jerk!" She screams, clenching her hands and blowing out a breath.

I can feel my heart in my throat and I just want to run to her and kiss her and tell her to stop doubting me. Just when I'm about to tell her she's wrong, Vince walks in and stops in his tracks.

"Is this another fight?" Arabella huffs and walks further into the classroom, leaving Vince to stare at me.

"I'm sorry Vince we won't be long." He smiles and puts his stuff on his desk.

"No problem! I need to speak with a student, anyway. Take all the time you need." He turns back around to leave and closes the door behind him. Taking a deep breath, I walk to Arabella.

"Teleiótita if you truly listened to all of my conversation with Chelsey then you would know that the only reason I was talking to her was because Taylor likes her. I told her a story about when he saved my life and she liked it. I was only trying to talk him up. Everything else about hooking up wasn't real. I told her I wasn't interested because I'm taken and she said she was only testing to see if I was a loyal friend. Nothing more. I've already learned my lesson from the last time." She doesn't say a word and I fear that she won't let this go.

"Why?" The question comes out so quickly and quietly I almost don't hear it.

"Why what?" I inch closer to her until I'm right behind her.

"Why me?" She turns around and looks up at me with the most beautiful eyes on this planet. Unshed tears shimmer in her questioning gaze and I just want to kiss her pain away.

"I thought I told you before, teleiótita. Because you are you and we are just us and that makes me the happiest man on the planet. You make me happier than I've ever been in so long… a happiness I figured I didn't deserve. Your beauty-"

"There's nothing beautiful about me." She says looking away.

Frustrated that she's not listening I take her face in my hands and kiss her. I know she will be mad and I know she may push me away, but I can't think of the words powerful enough to express how I'm feeling right now.

I kiss her lips softly pecking every inch of them and then I deepen the kiss angling my head to get the full extent and even then it's not enough. I tangle my hands in her soft full hair and pull her into me. I don't care if she can feel my arousal because I just want to feel her. After another minute, I pull back.

"If that kiss couldn't explain it well enough I don't know what will." Arabella steps back and touches her lips. She's shocked, but she doesn't look angry.

"You-you kissed me." I nod and watch her trace her lips before looking back up to me. Her lips look like pillows right now with how swollen they are.

"Can I kiss you again?" I ask cautiously. She nods her head slowly and walks towards me.

I peck her lips once and then twice and watch her reaction. Her eyes are closed, she's breathing slowly and there's not an ounce of fear, stress or pain on her face. She looks so serene.

I kiss her softly and lick at her lips. I don't want to overstep my boundaries, but I want to devour her right now. Kissing her again a little harder, I feel her hands slip up my chest and I moan out.

"Darien." My name sounds so sexy coming out of her I can't help grabbing her closer and plunging my tongue into her mouth.

She responds quickly and tries to kiss me back just as hard. She grabs my shirt and pulls me into her. I grind against her, rubbing my arousal into her stomach and she pushes her breasts against me. Lifting her up, I sit her down on a desk and stand in between her legs. I pull back for a split second to catch my breath and she's the one that pulls me back into her. She looks crazed, and she's crazed for me, and that makes me even crazier.

Something between a moan and a purr releases from her mouth and I bite her bottom lip because I've wanted to do that for so long. My lips are on her neck, biting her ear and then back on her lips. I can feel her hands gripping at my shirt and then they're under my shirt and on my skin.

My hand grips at her hair harder than before and I feel her inexperience peak as she keeps mashing her lips against mine. We keep colliding into each other making a mess of affection and I wouldn't have it any other way. Using my free hand, I wrap her leg around my back, and she follows with the other.

Pushing myself further into her. Her tongue slips out and accidentally licks my upper lip and I relish in the feeling. Our tongues tease each other slowly and our frantic hands slow down and everything in the world just slows down altogether so we can experience this. My hands snake up her shirt and hers move down to my hips.

"Oh wow."

Vince's voice pulls me from our kiss and Arabella jumps back, though she doesn't get far since she's sitting. I turn to see Vince leaning in the doorway with his arms crossed. I protect Arabella from his sight because she must be beyond embarrassed while I am feeling like the king of the world. The smile on Vince's face is infectious and I smile too. Arabella hides her face in my back.

"I'm glad to see everything is ok between you two, but I have to say I did not see this coming. Did you want me to leave?"

"NO!" She shouts out from behind me. Vince and I laugh lightly, and I pull her down from the desk.

"Well it doesn't matter really I have a class in twenty minutes." As soon as he finishes his sentence a student walks into the room. How long were we making out? We gather our stuff and meet Vince at the front of the class.

"Um..." Arabella looks up to Vince and bites her lip.

"No worries, I won't say a word. But I will say please leave that at home. I'm happy you two are... happy with each other and that's great because you're both good for each other but not in my classroom. Please." I can tell he's trying not to laugh again and so am I.

"Yes sir." Leaving his classroom, we walk to my car hand in hand allowing the silence to speak for us.

Eighteen

Overwhelmed

Arabella

Throughout the rest of the day my mind is reeling. It's hard to process what just happened between us. I keep replaying it in my mind repeatedly and it's still so hard to believe. It's like a dream, the best dream I've ever had.

"Teleiótita? We're at your house now." Darien says pulling the car to a stop.

I angle my body towards the window. On the outside it looks like I'm staring out the window, but I can barely see anything other than Darien kissing me. I can feel it, taste it, hear his groans and smell his cologne.

He touches my hand and my body heats, tingling in the part that shall never be named. I feel so hot right now and it's like Darien is the only cool drink of water that can quench this heat. Oh, my gosh, I want him so bad.

"Can I come in with you or do you think we should have some space first?" *Come in! Come in! You better get your gorgeous butt in my house! And on my bed and in my bathroom and on the couch!*

Where's Lydia when I need her? I could use some snide comments right now. Anything to get me to relax, even just a little. I try to take a breath, but he's filled the air with his cologne and his cologne reminds me of the kiss and the kiss reminds me of the fact that my body is so hot for Darien right now.

"You should leave." My voice sounds so steadier than I feel. "This is all too much. I'm not saying I didn't like it... it was just a lot to take in at once." He nods his head and gets out of the car to open my door.

I don't want him to touch me again. I don't trust myself to behave if he does. When he opens the door, I rush out and run up the steps to my house without turning around. Shutting the door, I lean against it and catch my breath. The farther I am from him, the easier it will be to cope.

And to breathe.

My phone vibrates, and I take it out of my bag. He texted me. Looking out the window, I can see he's sitting in his car.

I want to be in that car. I want to ride in that car... I want to ride him! Ride! Ride! Ride!

Who the hell is this sex-crazed girl in my head? We've never met before! She's insane!

Darien: I understand why you ran. I don't think I would have been able to just hug you. I hope I can call you tonight?

Arabella: I will call when I'm ready.

Darien: Ok. I miss you already.

Arabella: Stop acting so desperate. It's a turnoff.

Darien: So I turn you on?

Arabella: Isn't that the understatement of the century...

Darien: It's just nice to see you admit it finally. BTW, I have scratch marks all over my chest.

Arabella:... I didn't know... I'm so sorry.

Darien: Don't you DARE apologize. These marks are a badge of honor.

Arabella: You're such a loser.

Darien: Am I your loser?

Arabella: You don't belong to me.

Darien: After what we just did... I think I do.

Arabella: Go take a cold shower.

Darien: Only if you join me.

Arabella: You're pushing it, Darien.

He doesn't respond for a few seconds and I feel my heart race. This is bad. This is so very bad.

Darien: You're right. I'll talk to you tonight.
Arabella: Yeah.

I look out the window again and watch as he starts the car and drives off. Even from here I can see the smile on his face. When he's completely out of sight, I release a breath. Good. Now I can think and process what happened between us. What is happening?

"Why do you look like you saw a ghost?" Screaming, I turn to see Adam in the living room. I try to compose myself; I really do, but I just can't.

"Um... I–I. What are you doing?"

Excellent job! Deflect the question. As if he can't smell the hormones radiating off of you. This new horny girl needs to shut the hell up.

"I'm watching T.V." I smile and bite my lip, my eyes searching for anything else to look at than my brother right now.

"Shouldn't you be at work? Grease monkey?" I say smiling warily. Only I'm allowed to call him that.

All three of my brothers graduated from college with honors. Adam wants to own a garage and rebuild cars. Adrian works at some big-time business company and Alec is a fitness trainer.

Each one of them is following their dreams and succeeding. They'll be living with us until next year when they buy their own place. They wanted to stay with me until I graduated to make sure I was safe. I love them so much.

"I finished early. Besides, I make my own hours... what's up with the hickey on your neck?" I look at him and then touch my neck. Hickey?

"You have no idea, do you?" I shake my head and he laughs and turns back to the T.V. as I rush to the hallway mirror and look for this apparent–HOLY CRAP! THIS THING IS SO HUGE! AND DARK! And kinda sexy...

Adam walks up behind me and smirks.

"Aren't you supposed to be mad and want to kick this guy's butt?" Adam scoffs and throws an arm over my shoulder.

"Are you serious, Ari? You haven't had a boyfriend, let alone a friend in

God knows how many years and then suddenly this kid takes an interest in my baby sis and makes her laugh and smile? He makes you feel special and liked and that's ok with me. He can kiss you as much as he wants as long as that's all he's doing… and it's on the face… and I guess the neck."I shake my head and stare at the hickey.

"He's my first kiss Adam… it was all so… weird." He smiles wide and pulls me in for a hug.

"I am happy for you Ari just…" He pauses and I pull back.

"Just what?" I watch him hesitate with his words before he finally finds the right thing to say.

"Just don't hurt him Ari. The kid… I've never seen someone so invested in a person before. It's like he lives to be with you and that's cool with me but when those feeling aren't mutual, it can hurt like a… well a lot."

"But why would you think I would be the one to hurt him?" Adam sighs.

"Because you've never experienced such dedication and adoration from anyone other than us before. It's probably really overwhelming. And sometimes when you're feeling overwhelmed you lash out at those closest to you." I frown and touch the hickey.

"I don't mean to…"

"And it's not your fault. It's a defense mechanism so you don't let anyone get too close to hurt you… But not everyone will hurt you Ari ok? Just be careful with this guy." I nod and head upstairs to shower.

I can't believe he thinks that I would hurt Darien… if anything he'd be the one to hurt me… right?

***

"I'm happy you called me." Darien says over the phone. His voice is still sexy as ever. I roll my eyes and lie on my bed.

I've spent the past four hours going through the day and I still can't come up with a good enough reason for Darien to kiss me. I get that he likes me and may love me and he thinks I'm good-looking but it's all still so confusing.

"Yeah." What else am I supposed to say? I can barely think.

"So, I want you to meet my parents." I shoot up in the bed and choke on my saliva.

"What did you just say?" I'm still trying to catch my breath. Darien chuckles and speaks again.

"I want you to meet my parents. I've met your entire family and I think you'd like to meet mine." I scoff.

"Why?"

"I don't know… to get to know me better or something?" *I don't want to get to know you… I want to kiss you and kiss you and kiss you till I can't breathe.*

"I don't know Darien." He sighs and I feel bad.

"Well, just think about it. I'm not forcing you to do anything. I'm just suggesting it."

"Ok."

There's an awkward silence between us for a few seconds until the sex-crazed girl chants out some weird mantra. I try to ignore her and desperately search for Lydia's nasty voice, but I can't find it. Instead, I feet the words itch at the back of my throat. I'm feeling a sense of anxiety as I turn into Cady Heron from Mean Girls… word vomit.

"I want to kiss you again. I want to kiss your lips, your neck and every inch of your body. I want to touch you like I've touched no one before. I want you so badly it's scaring me… And I want you now. Like right now."

Again, there's silence before I hear the phone hit something, and then there's some cursing and fumbling around before Darien speaks again.

"Do you want me to come over? Because I'm getting dressed right now. Just give me a second." He sounds out of breath as the phone falls again and I hear a lot of shuffling.

I consider taking back every word I said, hanging up the phone and throwing it away, but I just sit on my bed and listen to the sounds of Darien rushing around his room. Eventually I hear him race down the stairs and yell out he'll be home late. The door slams shut, and I hear his car start, starting the race of my heart. I can't let him come up here. What would my parents think… what would my brothers do?

"Darien?"

"Yes! Yes, I'm here! And I'm driving to you right now. Give me ten minutes… I'm about to break a lot of laws tonight." Laughing, I play with the

134

ends of my hair and bite my lip.

"I don't think you should come over." Another pause.

"Do... do you want me to go back home?" He sounds so sad and disappointed right now.

"NO! I just... I don't want to sound slutty."

"Talk to me teleiótita." I hesitate and bite my lip again. What the hell is wrong with me? I should just push him away. This won't end well.

"I think we should stay in your car... not in public..." *As in I want to be like those girls in the movies and make-out with my not boyfriend in his car for endless hours.*

". Whatever you want. I'm like ten minutes away. Do you want me to meet you at the door?"

"I think my parents would appreciate that."

"Ok I'll be there soon." He hangs up the phone and I stare into my lap. I feel so different and dirty and stupid. I don't know what I'm doing, and Darien does. What am I getting myself into?

The doorbell rings making me jump up from my bed and rush to my mirror to fix my hair. Ten minutes passed faster than I thought it would. I haven't even changed out of my PJs! I grab a pair of sweats from the floor and the Michigan state shirt Adam brought me from his school.

"Arabella Darien is here." I hear my mom's voice and blush... if she really knew why Darien was here, I'm sure she wouldn't be so calm. Putting my hair up into a bun, I get dressed, grab my phone and head downstairs. I grab an infinity scarf to cover up the hickey he gave me. Darien is waiting at the front door and he can't stop moving. It's like he just keeps pacing back and forth. He looks like a mess and it's so sexy.

Actually, he looks just like he did that day he slept in and almost missed picking me up. His hair is messy, his shirt crushed, his sweats a little dirty, but the difference is the way he's acting. It's like he's on the verge of exploding.

I'm sure he wants to explode in you! Yay for explosions!

This girl really needs to get a damn grip!

When he sees me, his eyes widen and he licks his lips. *Oh my gosh how am I going to survive the night?* He greets me at the stairs and touches my waist careful to keep his hand there since we are in plain sight of my family.

"You've never worn your hair up before." His voice is breathless and low and so seductive.

"It's a mess and I can't be bothered with it right now." He nods, but it's like a robotic movement. His eyes scan my body twice before his mouth twitches and his grip on me tightens.

"We should get going… I don't think I can stop touching you and your parents are watching." I nod and say goodbye to my family before following him to his car. Once we are both in, I can feel the tension. It's thick and tightening around my throat. I don't know what I'm doing, and my mind isn't clear… all I know is that I want Darien's lips on me.

"There's this park close by that I can stop at. There won't be many people there at this time of the night." His voice is tense, and I watch as he squeezes the wheel in his hands.

He's squeezed our body like that, and he better do it again! I can't disagree with that thought.

I rest my head against the seat and try to calm my heart, so it won't burst. This is too intense, he's too intense and sexy and experienced. He shouldn't be rushing to my house at nine in the evening to make out with me in his car. He should be out with his friends partying and drinking and dancing and whatever other things they do at parties. He should have a pretty girl on his arm that is normal and smart and funny and has everything he's ever wanted. He should be anywhere else than with me.

"Teleiótita do you like the view?" My eyes focus on what's outside and I gasp at the stars. They look so pretty, and the trees are so tall and lush and the area is so peaceful and this is such a romantic moment… why is he spending it with me?

Oh, come now little freak, he's just trying to have sex with you! First, it's starts with false adoration, then it's a kiss and soon you'll be so addicted to him that sex will be right around the corner. And once he's done with you… once he's wasted you away then you will not only be a freak ,but you will be a slut too.

Damn Lydia is such a witch. She's a viciously honest brat, and I got what was coming to me… the truth. Isn't this what I knew all along? That he was

Overwhelmed

only using me? That whatever he feels for me isn't real?

"Arabella... We don't have to do anything right now if you're having second thoughts." He says cautiously.

I look Darien up and down and know that even though he's just trying to take my feelings into account, with the huge bulge in his pants he's definitely hoping I haven't changed my mind.

"I'm ok. I was just... thinking." Darien groans, turns off the car and undoes his seatbelt. Unbuckling mine, he takes my face into his hands.

"Don't think teleiótita, just feel." He kisses me softly but already I feel like it's not enough.

I kiss him back harder than before and I hear an animalistic sound come from his throat. His hands tangle into my hair and he breaks the elastic holding it up.

And he said he liked my hair up.

When my hair falls loose, fanning out all around my face, he pulls me even closer and bites my lip. I think he enjoys doing that. I place my hands on his chest and run them up and down his torso. He's so warm and chiseled and sexy. I don't realize it, but somehow I've ended up on top of him and he's reclined his seat back.

Kicking off my shoes I continue to play with his chest and kiss him fully. Our tongues thrash against each other for a few seconds before they almost mold together. Darien keeps lifting his hips and I feel his hands travel down my face and straight to my butt. He squeezes it hard and pulls it towards him.

He wants us to grind on him! We will grind! WE WILL GRIND!

I follow sex-crazed girl's advice and push against him.

"Ah!" He rasps out. Darien pulls back from our kiss to throw his head back. He's clenched his eyes and bites his lip... he really likes this. I continue to push against him and he uses his hands to get me into a rhythm. Each time I move forward on it, he lifts his hips to meet me. I think I don't know any other word than sexy right now. I watch his Adam's apple bob with each movement and I bend down to lick it.

"FUCK!" He calls out, his voice sounding deeper.

I find I kinda like it when he screams profanities because of our dirty doings.

I continue to lick it and bite it and then I'm biting all over his neck and licking him like a dog.

And you called him the puppy.

I suck on the space between his neck and his shoulder and his nails grip my butt harder than before. I watch in amusement as his face scrunches up and he pants heavily. Darien pushes me to grind on him harder and faster than before that I lose pace. His eyes open for a split second and I see they almost look black they are so dilated.

He kisses me hard and takes one of his hands to hold my head in place while the other goes to my hip. The part that shall never be named is so tingly it almost hurts right now and my breasts feel heavy suddenly. My nails scratch at his chest and I bite him back like he's been doing to me. In a matter of seconds Darien is bucking his hips up into mine and kissing me so hard I think my lips will bruise.

I don't what the hell he's doing, but it's starting to feel like too much. I try to pull back, but he won't let me go. I can hear his breathing picking up even faster than before and he takes both hands to force me to grind as hard as I can on him.

His eyes open again, and I see him watch my breasts move like he's hypnotized. I feel a weird zap in the part that shall never be named and I bite my lip as wetness pools in between my legs. My body is so hot right now and Darien looks like he wants to combust and then he screams out.

"Holy fuck Arabella!"

What the hell just happened?

I pull back to see his eyes clenched again and his heartbeat hammering in his neck. When he finally opens his eyes, he blushes hard.

"Oh, Arabella." His voice sounds so different when he's turned on. He lets go of my hip and I can see his nail marks embedded in it.

"I'm… I didn't mean to… It was all happening so fast and then I couldn't control it."

"What are you talking about Darien?" If possible, his face goes even redder, and he glances down between us. We're both wearing sweats but while mine

Overwhelmed

are semi dry, his are not. HOLY CRAP!

"Did you just... I mean did you? Just-"

"I'm so sorry Arabella! I didn't want to! I was trying to hold it back! But then you started grinding and biting and licking and sucking and I just lost control. It was the most erotic thing I've ever experienced."

He just... in his pants... because of us! WE ARE SUPREME! WE ARE SUPREME! SUCK ON THAT LYDIA!

I giggle. I giggle because this is crazy, and he looks so sexy right now and I feel so hot and I don't know what else to do.

"You're not mad?" He asks sounding like a scared little boy.

"Why should I be mad? I mean, not only did I have my first kiss, but we've already made it to second base all in one day! I feel a little delusional, but I'm not mad." I say sounding giddy.

I get off his lap and sit back in the passenger seat. Darien fixes his seat back into its proper position and takes out some tissues. He looks at me, then the tissues, and blushes again.

"I'll be right back." I nod and look out the window, so I won't stare at him. When he comes back in he doesn't start the car. Smart choice... because we should talk.

"So... that was intense." *Wow Arabella way to sound stupid.*

"Yeah... I didn't expect things to escalate the way they did... do you regret any of this?" He's acting shy suddenly and it makes me nervous.

"No, I don't regret it at all. I don't think we should do that again... not for a while, but I'm ok with kissing." Again, with the whole my voice sounding steadier than I feel thing.

I am? Since when was I ok with it? I am not ok with it! Tell him you are not ok with it!

"That's fine with me. We'll go at whatever pace you want. I don't want you to feel rushed." I nod again and bite my lip.

He bit our lip. He bit our lip a lot.

This sex-crazed girl really needs to chill out.

"Ok." I say smiling softly. Darien smiles, kisses my lips once more and starts the car.

I would have told him I still didn't think what we were doing made any sense. I would have told him I figured this would end soon. I would have also said that I didn't feel well enough to receive his kisses, let alone his affection. But I don't. I say nothing else because I'm too scared.

I'm scared on the inside out and I'm feeling things I never thought I would have to experience and I don't know what to do about it anymore. I'm just so overwhelmed.

Nineteen

Opening Old Wounds

Darien

I drove Arabella home, and she gave me a peck goodnight. I wanted more, but I chose not to act on it because of everything we had done so far. In most cases I would have said goodnight to the rest of her family but I figured, what with the huge wet stain on my crotch, that they wouldn't want to see me.

Driving home I replay our make-out session in my head, and I get aroused all over again. My God! That was the hottest thing I have ever done with any girl before and I'm including sex. The way Arabella touched me and scratched me and bit me and then she licked me and damn it if I couldn't control what happened after that.

My phone vibrates and I plug it into my car so I can answer it hands free.

"Hello?" My voice sounds so raspy, probably from all of that yelling and groaning. I want to turn this car around and repeat everything with Arabella all over again.

"Hey Darien it's Taylor."

"What's up?" I hear a giggle in the background and presume he's at another party.

"I just want to thank you for talking to Chelsey for me. I didn't know you would tell her that story, but I really appreciate it."

"Yeah no problem. I figured honesty was the best way to go." Taylor laughs.

"Well it worked. So, thank you. I'll see you tomorrow?" *Tomorrow's Saturday... I want to spend the day with Arabella.*

"Nah I can't I'm busy."

"Oh yeah, that girl… yeah I get you. No problem. Just message me every once in a while so I know you're alive." I laugh at that and shake my head.

"Yeah sure."

"See ya."

"Bye." He hangs up the phone and I pull into my driveway. I'm so hard I don't think I can get up. Just great. I dial Arabella's number and it rings four times before she picks up.

"Darien?"

"Teleiótita."

"Hi." She sounds so shy and cute and I want to kiss her again.

"Hey." I wouldn't exactly say the silence between us is awkward as it is more charged with sexual tension mainly on my part.

"So you called because?" I laugh at her sass and close my eyes to the sounds of her breathing. I love that even though we just did something that has drastically changed our relationship, she hasn't changed a bit.

"I wanted to hear your voice." I hear her sigh and smile.

"Oh, come on Darien it's only been, what, thirty minutes since we last saw each other?"

"Thirty of the longest minutes of my life."

"You're so cheesy."

"Thank you. So, what are you doing tomorrow?" I ask, trying to see if she'd involve me somehow.

"Not sure. Maybe just hang out at my house. Why? Did you have something planned?"

"No, I just want to be with you." Again she scoffs

"Don't you have a life?"

"Well, my life was comprised of parties, girls and sex so if you want me to go back to that then–"

"No! Ok. Ok you win… what would you want to do?"

"Do you want to go for a walk?"

"In public?"

"That's usually how it goes, teleiótita." I can sense the hesitation in the way she's breathing. She doesn't want to be seen in public with me. But I don't know what the big deal is anymore.

"Oh…"

"Why don't you want us to be in public?"

"It's not you Darien–"

"And it's not you either, Arabella. There is absolutely nothing wrong with you. Please let's just go for a walk."

She doesn't answer immediately, and I allow her to wait because I know she's just contemplating if she wants to be seen or not.

"Can I wear a hat?"

"Absolutely not. I want to see all of your face." She huffs and I laugh because she is so damn adorable.

"Sunglasses?" *all right Darien this is where you compromise.*

"Only if it's sunny out."

"Fair enough… so are you home yet?"

"Yeah but I'm sitting in my driveway."

"Why?" I look down at my semi hard little friend and sigh.

"Just thinking." She hums and it sounds so coming from her.

"I see… you have a hard on and don't want your parents to see it."

"Yup. How did you guess?"

"Happens to my brothers all the time." I listen as Arabella laughs, she laughing so hard she snorts. I've never heard such happiness. The sounds of another's laughter ring in my ears but I push her away. All I need it Arabella now.

"I don't doubt that."

"Well, I'm going to go to bed. It's almost eleven. Goodnight, Darien." I can't help sighing at how sexy her voice sounds right now.

"Goodnight teleiótita." She hangs up and I decide I am somewhat decent enough to leave the car.

Getting out and opening the front door as quietly as possible I try to sneak my way upstairs, but my parents are too smart for that.

"Darien could you come here for a second?" Stepping down from the stairs, I head to the kitchen where I know they are waiting.

"What's up?" My father motions for me to sit down and I do so slowly. There's something going on.

"Darien we've been told about your suspension." *Yeah and it's been over with so why bring it up?*

"Ok?" Why are they acting so weird for?

"Well, sweetie, I just want to know whether we will need to–"

"No, we don't need to move. Trust me what happened was justified."

"And what exactly happened?" I look at both of my parents and think of plenty of lies to tell them, but I side with the truth.

"Some kids in my class were saying some rude things about Arabella–"

"Yes, that girl you like." Mom fills in. I smile softly at her and continue.

"Yeah so I just would not sit there and let them insult her like that, so I told them off. Used some poor language, threw a chair and got suspended. Nothing big this time." Both of their heads nod in unison and my dad smiles.

"So, about this girl." Dad drawls.

"What about her?"

"Well, when are we going to meet her?" I shrug and lean back in my chair.

"I've given her the opportunity so now I will wait and see. I don't want to rush her with anything."

"Is she nervous about meeting us? Have you met her parents? What is she like? What's her major?" Mom asks too many questions at too late a time.

"Yeah, I've met her family, they're great and Arabella just doesn't want to give you guys the wrong impression about us." Both of their eyebrows raise, and I wonder if they rehearse these facial expressions.

"And what impression may that be?" Dad asks sipping his coffee.

"That we're a couple…"

"But aren't you a couple?" Mom asks, leaning forward.

"Not exactly… it's hard to explain."

"Ok… well we would like to meet her. She is your first girlfriend in a long time, Darien."

"Yeah, I know... and don't call her my girlfriend in front of her ok? I'll talk to her about it." I get up to leave and dad raises a hand to stop me.

"Was there something else?" I ask, looking back at them.

"This New Year's, you didn't spend it alone..." A sharp pain hits me in the chest and I grit out a response.

"Yeah?" Mom gets up to hug me, but I step away from her. Her arms fall to her sides and she closes her eyes.

"We just thought it was nice to know that you might be—"

"I'm not. I just... Arabella and I just made up, and I wanted to be with her, but that changes nothing."

"Shouldn't it though sweetie? It's been five years—"

"I KNOW HOW LONG IT IS! JUST DROP IT!" I run up the stairs and slam my door closed. Holding my chest, I try to breathe like the doctor told me. I try not to think about the pain and the tears. About the flashing lights and the sirens. I try to think about anything that can calm me down. Immediately I see Arabella in my mind and the pain slowly eases.

I go to sleep with the image of her stamped behind my eyelids.

***

Waking up earlier than usual, I take a cold shower to wash away the haunting dreams. Why the hell would my parents bring up that... time for? We left it in the past because it was too painful to think about. It's still just as painful now as it was when it happened.

The feeling of the water hitting my skin is like icicles stabbing at the re-opened wound on my heart. Each droplet is another sting of pain, another flash of that night. But soon, as it always does, the pain subsides to a dull ache. One that I can push to the back of my mind and ignore.

Getting out of the shower, I towel off and ignore my reflection in the mirror. I don't want to be reminded of the haunted boy I used to be. I just want to fake happiness. I want a distraction. I need Arabella.

With my towel still wrapped around my waist, I head to my room and call my teleiótita. Glancing at the clock I see it's just eight in the morning, so she must be awake by now. After the third ring, she answers the phone.

"Hel–Hello?" Her voice sounds so sleepy that I feel stupid for calling her so early in the morning, but as the memories try to resurface, I decide that calling her was the best thing I could do.

"Good morning, teleiótita. Did you have a good sleep?" I hear some of her muttering and some shuffling before she answers me.

"Well, I was having a good sleep until you called." I can hear sirens blaring outside my window and another memory hits me.

Blue and Red lights were everywhere. Yellow tape tacked all along the surrounding area. The smell of alcohol that once brought pleasure now only brings nausea. Everything is so dark and yet I can see it just lying there. So still so peaceful, so d–

"Darien? DARIEN!" I jump at the sound of Arabella's voice and let go of the sheets I'm fisting. There's sweat on my forehead and down my chest and my vision is blurry.

"Sorry Belle. I'm listening."

"Is there something wrong?" I chuckle nervously at her question. What would she think of me if I told her? *No, you can't burden here with your problems when she's got so many of her own! Help her grow first and when you truly know she loves you then-*

"How many times do I have to keep calling out your name before you answer?"

"Oh sorry! I–my mind is all over the place."

"Do you want me to come over?" My throat closes up, but I force myself to speak.

"No. No, it's ok. I'll come to you. I'll be there soon. Is that ok?"

"Yeah it's fine… and Darien,"

"Yes, Belle?"

"Whatever's bothering you, no matter how I act or what I say, what we did… its brought us closer right?"

"Yeah, it has."

"Good, then you know you can talk to me right?"

"Huh?" She's being sincere with me. No attitude, no snarky comments, just pure sincerity… I swear this girl is making me fall harder and harder every day.

"I'm just saying that even though we are messed up and I have some many issues on my own... I'm here if you need me Darien. Cause... I like you. And I want to be there... and it's probably the lack of sleep talking but yeah." Tears well up in my eyes and I breathe out slowly so I don't sound too choked up.

"Thank you, teleiótita. I love you."

"You're welcome, Darien. I'll leave the door unlocked for you." She hangs up and I wipe at the few tears that ran down my face. I am so in love with this girl.

I get dressed quickly and leave the house. Jumping in my car, I stop by Denny's getting Arabella some breakfast. It's the least I can do since I woke her up so early. Since I have no idea what she would want to eat I just get her a range of pancakes, French toast, eggs, bacon, sausage, toast, biscuits, and both orange and apple juice. If we can't finish the food ourselves, I know her brothers will.

I arrive at her house twenty minutes later and walk in. It's so funny how houses can be houses, but a home is always a home. And my teleiótita's house is truly a home. With a trimmed green lawn with a large tree smack dab in the middle and a tire swing. The outside of the house seems modest but it's the inside that's the difference.

They haven't even lived here a year, and it seems like she grew up in this place. There are pictures of her family all along the walls with inspirational words lining each step and along the staircase. They've painted the walls warm colours that welcome each entrant and make you feel at ease. It's so comforting in this home... not at all like my house.

"Good morning Darien." Looking to my right, I see Mr. and Mrs. Wilson sitting comfortably on their couch in the living room. I can see now that the T.V. is on, but I can't hear anything playing.

"Good Morning Mr. and Mrs. Wilson." I've always tried to be as charming as possible with Mr. Wilson. It's obvious that Arabella is a daddy's girl and I want him to see that I love his daughter more than anything.

"Come on, kid, stop calling us that. You make us sound like my parents. It's just Paul and Sasha cool?" Paul says casually. I smile and nod.

"Got it. So, I brought Belle some breakfast, where should I put it?" Sasha points to the kitchen.

"Leave it on the table. You're in luck today, the boys went to the beach with some friend's last night and they still haven't come in. There's a chance that you will eat in peace."

"Cool. We'll see how long that lasts." Both parents laugh at my joke and I feel the pain completely fade away. I place the food on the table and take out some plates and cups. When I'm finished, I turn to Arabella's parents and blush.

"Do you mind if I?–"

"Isn't it so sweet of him to ask if he can go upstairs, Paul? It's rare you see a boy like that anymore." Paul nods and waves me the ok to head upstairs.

I've never been in Arabella's room before and as I climb the stairs, I get anxious. Being in her room means we'll be behind a closed door. That also means that we'll be by her bed. The bed that she sleeps on and hopefully dreams about me in. The bed that I could easily push her down on and ravish her body in. I pause mid step and rethink whether I should go up there. Last night is still fresh in my mind...

"What are you doing?" I look up from my feet and see my teleiótita, my beautiful, wonderful girl standing with her arms crossed, effectively raising her top and showing me her stomach. She's wearing another pair of sweats and a loose-fitting shirt that has Mickey Mouse on it. Her hair isn't up today.

"I was trying to figure out whether I would go to your room." She rolls her eyes and pushes past me.

"You chose too late." I follow behind her to the kitchen. I'm watching her butt so much I don't realize she's stopped and bump into her.

"What's the matter?" I ask, pulling at my shirt so my arousal isn't so noticeable. She points to the breakfast I set up and I smile.

"Do you like it?" She nods her head and wordlessly sits at the table.

"I wasn't sure what you liked, so I got you a bit of everything." She nods again and serves herself some food. I pour out a mixture of both orange and apple juice and serve myself.

"Did you want us to serve you out some food Sasha?" I ask her parents. I hear her light laughter and figures that's a no.

"We'll eat whatever you leave, Darien. Thank you for offering." I shift back in my seat and catch Arabella staring at me.

"Teleiótita?" She blinks rapidly and shakes her head.

"Sorry. I was just having a hard time believing you were real." Smirking, I stand up and walk to her side of the table. Her eyes watch me cautiously, but her body language is open and inviting. Leaning down to her, I watch her eyes as I kiss her lips, once, twice, three times and pull back.

"That wasn't too much, was it?" She shakes her head no and I return to my seat. I'm so sure I heard her mutter, "It wasn't enough," but maybe that's just wishful thinking on my part.

"So what's your favourite breakfast meal?" I ask as I dig in to my pancakes.

"Stuffed French Toast." Her mouth is full of food and she's already got a bit of syrup on her shirt and she's so damn beautiful.

"I'm glad I bought so much then." Arabella laughs and my heart soars.

"I don't know why you did it but thank you."

"I thought it was a gracious way of saying sorry for waking you up so early on a Saturday." Her eyes roll and she sighs in pleasure.

"You should say sorry more often." She drinks the juice I made her and moans in pleasure. It's not as loud as the moans she was giving me last night, but it still turns me on.

"Sorry." I reply to her comment. Husky, low and seductive, that's how my voice sounds and I feel so stupid and yet so very turned on. Her head slowly rises from her food and she watches me through narrowed eyes.

"You ok there, Darien?" I clear my throat and sit up straighter.

"Yup… there was uh–there was something in my throat." Belle smirks and finishes her food.

"Thank you for the breakfast Darien, it was delicious."

"You're welcome, teleiótita. Just watching you eat has made my morning." Her blush is faint but still apparent and I hold back a groan of annoyance that her shirt is covering her breasts this time. I'm such a pervert. *That's something that hasn't changed since...*

"Are you ready to go on our walk?" She looks down at her shirt and frowns at the syrup stains.

"Let me go change first." She gets up and I get up with her. I'm suddenly very uneasy about letting her leave my sight. *You were clingy with her too. Look where that got you.*

"Can I come with you?" Her mouth drops open, and she blushes even harder.

"No, you can't you pervert!" I raise my hands in defense and shake my head.

"Not in that way, Belle. I just want to be near you." Something in the way her posture changes and her body loosens, tells me she will give in.

"Ok… just don't peak." I beam at her acceptance.

"No peaking." She takes my hand and leads me upstairs to her room. When she pushes the door, I notice it's clean. Her bed is straightened, there're no clothes scattered anywhere and not even a crumb on her dresser. Everything is in a proper place and with the sunlight streaming in it looks so much like her. Put together, clean and organized. Arabella keeps holding my hand till we reach her bed and let's go.

"So yeah, this is my room." I nod and walk around. She's got a bunch of souvenirs from the unfamiliar places she stayed. There's a foam finger sporting Texas State, a mini Statue of Liberty from New York, an "I love Virginia" teddy bear and a Georgia "The Peach State" license plate.

"You like souvenirs, huh?" I hear some muffled sounds and figure she's changing now.

"Yeah, I travel so much that I need something to remember each place by. You know besides the horrible memories." I nod as I trace the different colored lines on an enormous world map hanging on her wall.

"Do you think you will leave again?"

"Who knows, maybe?" My heart stops at the thought of Arabella leaving me. What would life be without her? I'd be miserable again… I'd be empty. *Isn't it safer that way?*

"Do you want to leave?" I ask quietly. I feel a hand on my shoulder and I turn to see Arabella is wearing another loose-fitting shirt, similar to her other one except this one is low cut. I don't care whether she wore this for me, I love it.

"Why ask me a question like that?" Her eyes are wide and she's trying to look upset, but I know better.

"Because I love you and the thought of you leaving is a little terrifying." She sighs and runs her hand up my chest and rests it on my face.

"Darien eventually we will go our separate ways. That's how life works."

"Well then, I will enjoy life right now. And I will hold on to you for as long as I can." She smiles and plays with my collarbone.

"If it were up to you, you'd never let me go, would you?"

"It's not up to me."

"But would you?"

"I'd never let you go, Arabella." She mews and I pull her in for a kiss. It's slow and affectionate and I want her to feel just how much I love her. As usual she pulls back, her face flushed, her lips plump, her eyes dilated and sparkling. She's so beautiful.

"Let's get going." She grabs her bag and a pair of sunglasses and we head downstairs.

When we get outside I open her door for her and thank God that it's not that sunny today. Opening the car door for her as I always do, I get a look down her shirt when she sits down. Closing the door quickly, I tell myself to get a grip and join her in the car. Sitting beside her, I start the car and begin the drive to the park.

"I hope you know you never covered your eyes once when we were in Disneyland."

"I–I was happy then–"

"And no one looked at you funny once."

"–I kept my head down most of them time–"

"I'm sure I heard at least five people compliment your eyes and you responded with a thank you."

"–You just don't understand Darien."

"What is there for me to understand, teleiótita? All of this torment you put yourself through... the majority of it is at your own hands." I watch in my peripheral as she drops lower into her chair.

"I don't know what you're talking about." I take her hand in mine and kiss it.

"Yes, you do. The bullying stopped at school and you still act like the world is against you. Even when people are working for you, you push them away. All for what?"

"You don't know Darien." Her voice is indistinct, but I can hear her all the same.

"What don't I know, teleiótita?"

"I–I… forget it." I pull into a parking lot and stop the car.

"No, I will not forget it Arabella. This is something that has been bothering me for months now. What don't I know?"

"It's… people… they don't always have to talk to express how they feel." Taking off my seatbelt, I turn to give her my full attention.

"Meaning?"

"Meaning facial expressions, body language, hand gestures, all of that can describe how someone feels. Like you. I may not like to admit it out loud, but the way you look at me and smile and touch me, it's a simple expression of your love." She pauses and wipes at her eyes. "But with everyone else… the whispers and the glares they speak so loud."

"Arabella not everyone is saying something bad about you."

"You don't know that."

"Yes, I do! I'm in class with a good amount of them and yes at one point they were bad-mouthing you but now, they've moved on. You're different, so what? They don't care anymore."

"I want to stop talking about this."

"But Arabella–"

"I WANT TO STOP TALKING ABOUT THIS." She shouts, slamming her hand against the car door. I start the car and continue driving to our destination. We don't say a word to each other the rest of the ride.

Twenty

The Truth Hurts

Arabella

When we arrived at the park, all I wanted to do was go home. I didn't like where our conversation was going because it was getting too emotional. It was too much and too intense for something that may not even last that much longer.

"So, there's a cool trail just up ahead." I nod and take Darien's hand. He made me leave my glasses in the car, but thankfully there aren't many people in the park right now, so I don't have to worry about any ridicule.

"I'm glad you're not wearing those stupid glasses."

"You made me leave them." He smirks and wraps an arm around my shoulder.

"Well, I'm glad you listened." I can't help resting my head on his chest as we continue to walk. It's peaceful and there's so many birds flying around and chirping softly. I wouldn't mind coming back here.

"How did you find this place?"

"GPS." I hit his side and we both laugh. He's such a jerk... my jerk... whether or not I like it.

Stop trying to fake it! You know you LOVE it!

I've named this sex-crazed girl SCG, because I can be unoriginal every once in a while.

"Do you like it here so far?" I nod against his chest and close my eyes, allowing his body to direct me.

Over the course of eight hours I realize that although my first kiss and going to second base came as a surprise, I can't expect much more.

I can't psyche myself into believing that anything good and long-lasting will come of this relationship. I can't even fully admit that Darien and I are basically... well... we're dating. I've never even had a boyfriend before, and everything seems to happen so fast...

But isn't that how life is you little freak? Wonderful things come and go faster than the bad. The bad things last long. The nasty things are never ending. The awful things are endless. The good... it will blow up in your face sooner than you know it.

I shiver at the sound of Lydia's voice. She comes whenever she pleases now and says whatever she deems fit. She knows no bounds and has no filter. She's part of what I thrive on... how sick is that? I inwardly give my head a shake and focus on this... oh man this is meant to be romantic isn't it? Is this a date?

"Is this a date, Darien?" He looks down at me with a full-blown smile and eyes glittering in the sunlight.

"It's whatever you want it to be, teleiótita." *What if I want it to be a date?*

"All right... then it's just a walk." His hold on my shoulders tightens.

"Glad to know that's what we're doing." As we walk further down the path, the trees get larger and their branches twist above us creating a very romantic archway above us.

"People have weddings in this place?" Darien takes my hand and leads me over a bridge and straight towards the faint sounds of music. Passing some more trees, we happen upon a small wedding of maybe fifty people. There's a rustic feel to their décor with paper lanterns hanging in the trees and leading to two posts where the bride and groom are standing. There's thin white runway going down the middle and everyone is sitting on benches angled to face the wedding party. It looks so beautiful.

"Can we stay?" I ask quietly. Darien pulls my hand forward and we sit on a bench in the very back. I feel so underdressed compared to everyone here. Darien pulls me into him and kisses the top of my head and I get that warm and fuzzy feeling again.

We love the warm and fuzzies! We love it!

SCG can be such a hand full.

The bride is wearing an off-white lace gown with a scoop neckline and a low back. It fits her body perfectly and still leaves room for her to move around. She has a little of a train that adds to her elegant look and a bouquet of white Amaryllises. She looks so stunning. Her hair is up in a side bun and she's wearing a birdcage headpiece that perfectly frames her face. I can see her engagement ring from back here and man is it a rock! With minimum makeup and pearl earrings she looks exactly as I would want to when I get married; Elegant, beautiful and classy.

The bridesmaids are wearing dusty pink knee-length dresses with daisy bouquets and cowboy boots. Now that I look hard enough I can see the bride is wearing cowboy boots. The groomsmen are wearing beige pants with suspenders and crisp white shirts with brown and white checkered bow ties. The groom... He looks so happy in a tan suit, red bowtie and a big smile.

"Is this the wedding you'd like to have?" Darien asks me. I look up to him and then back to the wedding and nod.

"Yeah, I'd want it to be secluded like this. No one to see me. No one to bother me."

I didn't mean to say that. I meant to say that I loved nature and its natural beauty. I love how they used their surroundings to create an enchanting atmosphere. I love the bride's dress and I love everything about this place.

"You shouldn't be happy about wanting to hide away teleiótita. If I could marry you I'd want everyone to see how beautiful you would look. I would want to make the world jealous of our love."

"You're so cheesy."

"You've already used that line, Belle."

"Well, I'm using it again because it's true." We both laugh quietly and carefully get up to leave the wedding. It's their special moment it's only fair they don't walk down the aisle to see two random people crashing their wedding.

We linger around the wedding area still because it's just so beautiful that before we know it, the ceremony is over and people are leaving. Darien keeps me entertained talking about his friend Taylor and the silly things he's don–

"Oh, what a coincidence." I know that voice. I seriously know that voice. Turning around, I see Lydia walking towards us with some auburn-haired guy on her arm.

"Were you crashing the wedding because you know you'll never have one of your own?" She asks snidely. I blink a few times just to assure myself that she isn't saying this in my head and that she is standing only a few feet away from me. But as I force myself to pinch my arm and I realize she is still standing there, I know it's real.

"Lydia… what are you doing here?" Darien asks for me. The man Lydia's with looks me up and down with a nasty smirk on his face and Darien's hold tightens on me.

"Well, I'm attending this wedding Darien honey. Remember, I invited you a few weeks ago, but you said you were busy? I didn't think this was your excuse. What was she the only girl available at the last minute?" She laughs to herself and the man chuckles too. But Darien is tensing which means he's getting furious.

"Please just leave us alone Lydia." I say as firmly as I can. Her eyes cut to me and she grinds her teeth.

"You know I'm getting very tired of you Arabella. And you know what pisses me off about you? Do you?"

"No." I answer meekly. She laughs loudly and marches right up in my face.

"I hate that you like to act like you're some innocent petty girl. Like you have no sin in the world. Like you just don't remember." I stare at her, confused and terrified all at once.

"Remember what?" I ask quietly. Darien tries to pull me behind but I shrug him off and try my hardest to be brave.

"Oh, you don't remember me. You don't. You pathetic petty bitch."

"Hey watch your damn mouth Lydia." Darien says stepping closer to me but I hold him back because there is something familiar about Lydia other than her snarky voice.

"What is there to remember Lydia?" I ask again.

"Browning? You don't remember me, huh? Lydia? HUH! Or maybe you'd remember this Bride of Frankenstein." And just like that, all the memories of my horrible childhood come rushing back. The teasing, the names, the bullying and the evil little girl with the perfect skin and the perfect hair and the perfect everything as the ringleader. Was Lydia that evil girl?

"That was you?" I can barely believe the words as they come out of my mouth.

"That's right, you freak. You thought you could tarnish my family name and run away with no retribution? You think I would just forget that you and your annoying little innocent self was always liked by everyone because you were so different, and no one cared about me? You think I would forget that!" Tears well in my eyes and I do something I never thought I would do. I slap Lydia right across the face. And then I do it again.

"You horrible, miserable bitch! What did I ever do to deserve such torment?" I try so hard not to scream because it will cause a scene but I guess slapping her was the start wasn't it? The man she's with covers his mouth in what I think to be astonishment, but then I hear him chuckle. What a loser!

"YOU WERE BORN! That's what you did! Everyone loved you! The prodigy! The gifted child! The beautifully unique little black girl! They even loved your name! My parents talked more about you than they ever did about me! MY OWN PARENTS!"

"How the hell is that my fault? I can barely remember anything from that age! All I remember was you ruining my life! You treated me so badly I had to move to a different state!" Darien holds me back because I'm about to hit her again.

"Shh teleiótita let's just get out of here. She doesn't deserve anymore. Don't waste your time on her." I let him lead me away from Lydia and the wedding party that seemed to gather around us. I let him completely control my every movement as my thoughts run wild.

We continue to walk for another hour until we hit another pathway that opens up to the Anaheim hills. I read about them when my parent's told me we were moving here. They're even more beautiful in person. And much more relaxing than the horror scene I was just in.

"Let's stop at this creek, teleiótita." At one point my feet began to ache, so Darien has been caring me on his back for the past ten minutes. When he lets me down I take off my shoes and socks and rest my feet in the water and Darien follows suit.

"Do you want to talk about what just happened?" Darien asks me calmly.

"No… I don't even know how to process it anyway." He nods and we both stare into the water.

"So what was up this morning?" I ask, leaning back on my hands to enjoy the sunshine. Darien is still silent, so I look over to him to see a solemn look on his face.

"Darien?" Touching his shoulder causes him to jolt forward, and he gasps out. I sit beside him unsure of what to do… it's always him that's in control and now the roles have reversed.

"Sorry my mind seemed to drift off. What did you ask me?" I lean into him and he responds by pulling us to lie down.

"What happened this morning?" With my head on his chest I can hear his erratic heartbeat and I get worried. There's something seriously bothering him.

"Something had come up." I've never experienced Darien being so closed off before. It worries me.

"You can't think you're allowed to pry into my life and not let me into yours. I told you I'm here for you so talk." Again, his breathing picks up and his hand grips my waist.

"I wouldn't know where to start…"

"How about the beginning?"

"Well… remember how I told you I was born in Hawaii?" I nod and hum a yes.

"Well at the time I wasn't an only child." His heartbeat is speeding up again. Something bad must have happened.

"I had a brother, an older brother actually. He was three years older than me."

"What was his name?"

"Hani it means happiness."

"Why doesn't your name sound Hawaiian?" He gulps and his hand moves up my waist as he plays with my exposed side.

"My birth name is Kai, it means from the sea. Ironic enough I loved surfing as a kid… but after… Let's just say I legally changed my name."

He pauses, and I let him have this time to breathe.

"Hani and I were like twins. You would have never guessed that he was older than me. Everything we did, we did together. He taught me carving, I taught him surfing, he taught me about girls' history and I taught him about world history. It sounds weird, but that–that's how it was. When I was fifteen, I was in love with this girl name Leilani. She was so beautiful and funny and she could surf like she was born to do it. But she never paid me any attention. In fact, she always played around with me, making me think if I tried harder, if I got closer, it would make her want me. I had asked my brother to help me win her affection…"

He pauses again and I can hear his heart race again. His nails dig in to my skin and sweat is breaking out on his body.

"It was New Year's Eve and there was this big beach party. I begged my brother to take me to the party because I knew Leilani would be there. We arrived when the moon was rising and the waves were strong. Everyone was dancing and drinking and enjoying the life. Even Hani and I drank. I just needed the liquid courage, Hani didn't care. Leilani had dared me to go out to the sea and catch a wave. I wanted to impress her, but I was too scared to do it, so Hani said he would. He was never as good a surfer as I was…" He's digging so deep into my side I'm sure he's pierced the skin and I will be bleeding soon.

"I told him I would do it with him because we were brothers and we stuck together. The waves we rough that night. The undertow was dangerous enough, but we were tipsy bordering on drunk and we didn't care. Leilani wasn't even paying attention, but I desperately wanted her to notice me.

In Her Eyes

Everyone was still dancing, not paying us any care, so it was just the two of us and the waves. Getting out there was tough, but I handled it fine. Hani wasn't doing so well."

"I didn't know he had so much more to drink than me. I didn't know that he wasn't confident in his surfing. I didn't know. The waves were crashing against us and soon easy surfing became a nightmare. I remember hearing Leilani's screams to get out. I remember seeing Hani's board flip up and I remember not seeing his body surface. I was already too drunk to know what I was doing myself, but when the waves got to me, I could swim through it. I grabbed onto my board and used to it keep me afloat. In that stupid drunken state I didn't realize that something was grabbing at my leg. I thought it was a shark or something so I kept kicking and kicking at it until it left me alone… that something was Hani. He was trying to pull himself up, but I kicked him down. It was a hard-enough blow that rendered him unconscious. He died in those waves. And it was my fault. I killed my brother."

I can feel his chest heave with a sob, and I hold him close to me. To think I thought I was going through something horrific and yet compared to Darien my problems are minuscule.

I thank God for my brothers; I don't know what I'd do without them.

"Darien you didn't know. How could you have known?"

"But I should have. I should have known he was only trying to rely on me as I've been on him for so many years. He was only eighteen teleiótita. He got into Julliard. Julliard! He was going to be a musician. He was so talented and he worked so hard and all of it was thrown away because I wanted to go to a stupid party to impress a stupid girl who ran away when she realized my brother was dead."

I feel his tears seep into my hair, and I continue to hold him. Even though the way we're lying down is a very awkward angle. Even though we are out in public and anyone could pass us. Even though I am a basket case all by myself, I hold him and let him grieve for a boy I never got to meet, but I wanted to.

"Darien I'm not good at these kinds of things, hell I don't even know how to handle my own problems but I know you can't blame yourself for what

The Truth Hurts

happened. You can't beat up on yourself for something out of your control–"

"Oh but you can?" I sit up from his chest and narrow my eyes.

"Excuse me?" Darien sits up as well and his face looks like he's bordering livid.

"You heard me, Arabella. At least I have every reason to be mad about what I may or may not have done because it killed someone, but what's your excuse? You lived your life getting bullied by people because you were different and it hurt you, but when the bullying stopped and you could finally move on what do you choose? You continue to berate yourself and degrade yourself and then blame it on everyone else. News flash Arabella, no one is laughing at you. No one is teasing you. No one is belittling you. It's all on you!" Tears well up in my eyes, but I refuse to let them fall. I won't let him bully me.

"You know nothing Darien!"

"I KNOW ENOUGH! I KNOW THAT YOU'VE BECOME SO ACCUSTOMED TO THE BULLYING THAT YOU MAKE UP THE WORDS AND THE STARES AND THE SNICKERING IN YOUR MIND! YOU WANT TO BE ABUSED! YOU WANT TO BE LAUGHED AT AND I HAVE NO CLUE WHY!"

"I DON'T KNOW EITHER!" I scream out the tears I was so adamant about keeping in already falling down my face.

"I don't know what's wrong with me! I don't know why I will imagine the pain! I just… I've become so used to it that when it stops I don't know what to do… who to trust."

"You can trust me teleiótita." He takes my hands in his but I pull them back.

"How do I know that? How do I know you won't turn your back on me or run to another girl because I won't sleep with you?–"

"None of that matters!"

"It matters to you, Darien! How can I trust you when you've already left me before?"

"You take a damn leap of faith! That's what love is Arabella! It's not all roses and sunshine! Its pain and heartache and trust and hope and believing in that person that they won't crush your heart. That they see the beauty in you even when you can't see it yourself!" Darien pants out his frustration and gets up to walk away from me.

I can't believe what he's saying. I don't even know what to say. It's all too much.

"Darien…"

"No. No, I can't. Arabella, I told you something that has haunted me for five years now. Something that I have regretted all my life. I told you this because I trust you and I love you and I believed that you could help me. But how the hell can you help me when you can't even help yourself?" He shakes his head and walks further away from me.

Scrambling, I get up and run to his side.

"I know I have problems and I know I'm not perfect but I can change! I can help you. I can love you!" His body shakes and I wrap my arms around him.

"Arabella you can't love me… not until you learn to love yourself." He unwraps my arms from his waist and turns to me. "We should get going."

Hanging my head I follow behind him as we walk back to his car. The once romantic trees high above now illustrating the hurt and confusion coiling around my heart. When we reach the car we don't say a word until he arrives at my house.

"Arabella I love you. I love you so much it hurts but I can't act as though I don't want that love back." I open my mouth to object but he smiles softly and I shut it just as quickly.

"I know that one day you will understand how you feel about me and when that day comes I will be right beside you… but until then… we shouldn't be together. Both of us need to re-examine our lives and where we want to go, what we want to be. You need to let go of this anger and pain that you inflict on yourself and I need to forgive myself for what happened to Hani… it's the reason I faked the accent all those months ago." He pauses and grips the steering wheel.

"After Hani's death I couldn't stand to be in Hawaii anymore and I begged my parents to move. So we did. But each place we moved to I tried to be someone other than Kai Petros because that way I would forget the pain. That way I could be someone who wasn't a killer, someone no one knew.

But I know that it doesn't change the past… and it doesn't change who I am." He sighs and angles his body towards me.

"When you know you're ready, for love, for new beginnings, for me… I'll be here. I love you Arabella and I can't wait to meet the new you. Take care of yourself. And the thing that happened with Lydia… don't let that bother you. She's a bitch, and she doesn't deserve your time or effort." He leans forward and kisses my lips before he pulls back and leaves me, mind, body and soul.

Twenty-One

Pain is So Damn Painful

Darien

Even after Arabella leaves my sight, I still can't move. The ache in my chest mixed with the sorrow from the memories of my brother's death leave me panting for breath.

I can't believe I did that. I broke up with Arabella. The one girl I've loved so much that I told the complete truth to and I break up with her. Groaning, I hit my head on the steering wheel. How could I be so stupid?

Starting the car, I leave her house and drive. It's still midday and I don't feel like going home so I just drive. Blurs of trees and buildings pass my vision as I speed down the highway. Nothing I think of can erase the never ending pounding in my chest.

I want to just go back to Arabella and profusely apologize for everything I said. I want to tell her I don't care about her messed up head and her insecurities. All that matters is that we're together. But that's where I know I'm wrong. What matters most to me is Arabella finally being comfortable in her skin. What matters to me is her absolute happiness that isn't clouded by anything. What matters to me is her freedom from herself.

I park the car and look out to where I've stopped. The beach.... I get out of the car and walk towards the shore. This place has haunted me for years,

I detest the one thing I've loved so much. I watch as two men surf against the waves and the critiquing immediately begins.

Even when I don't want to do it, even when I haven't touched a board in years. It's like I can't stop that part of me from reacting. I walk closer to the water, still partially observing the surfers and their pathetic attempts to "catch the waves". I don't even feel the water lick at my feet as I walk further into the sea.

I've thought about killing myself more than once, but I shut those thoughts down because I know it would disappoint Hani if I did. There isn't a day that goes by that I don't miss him and our bond. The water reaches my waist and I continue to venture in and I think about the joyful times I had with Hani.

Flashback

"Hey bro don't go wandering too deep yeah? If the sharks get you I will have to go fishing with a spear and you know I have a date with Kalani tonight."

I laugh at Hani's joke and continue my swimming. Hani and I always come to the beach when we finish school. It's only a five-minute walk from our house and we are old enough to take care of ourselves.

"Hani when you go to Julliard what am I supposed to do?" Hani shakes his head and jumps in the water with me.

"I haven't even auditioned yet bro relax." He swims beside me and dunks his head under the water before he emerges again and floats on his back.

"Yeah but come on Hani don't be lolo we both know you will make it. You're amazing. What'd the teach call you?"

"A prodigy."

"Yeah, a prodigy that means like the best yeah?" I float with him and we let the waves move us.

"Yeah, I guess. But I'm not rushing nothing. I'm only seventeen and I love it at home. I just want to enjoy the now, yeah? Ohana remember that."

"Ohana." We continue to float around until the sunsets and our skin prunes.

End of Flashback

Tears fill my eyes as I float on the waves like Hani and I used to. Even though I'm fully dressed, I've still mastered it well enough to glide on the water. I let the waves carry me back and forth, mimicking the feeling when my mom would rock me to sleep. I close my eyes and imagine I'm back in Honolulu again with my grandpa and grandma or my kupunakane and mykupunawahine. My mom would cook Lau lau and my dad would struggle to pick up the native tongue.

His family is from Greece, and he met my mom when he was attending a wedding in Hawaii. He ended up skipping the wedding so he could spend all his time with her. They married a year later and had Hani a year after that and me three years later. He's always had a hard time picking up our language since he's so used to speaking Greek and English. He and mom raised Hani and I to speak English first, then Hawaiian and Greek. We're trilingual.

I remember during the summer of Hani's eighteenth year… his last year of life; we would all have family dinners more often than usual since he would be away. Hani and I would help set up the table, while mom and grandma cooked. Dad would clean the kitchen and grandpa would watch T.V. and we'd all sit together and eat like a family.

Flashback

"Kai will you pray?" *I nod to kupunawahine and bow my head.*

"Dear God we thank you for the sun, the moon and the family. We thank you for our food, for our love and for the waves. Bless this dinner and bless kupunawahine and makuahine for preparing this food. Amen." *Everyone says amen and we dig in.*

"Keikikane are you packed and ready for your audition?" *Hani nods at grandma and grins.*

"I'm ready. I know I can ace this."

"We all do Hani." *Mom responds.*

I'm excited for Hani to get into this music school but when he's gone what am I supposed to do? I will miss him.

"Don't be sad, joke. Your brother will always be with you no matter how far."

"Yes, grandma." *Her face screws up at the English version of her name.*

"What have I said about calling me that? Your mother and father like English, yeah? With the Greek stuff, yes? You boys will be very important wherever you go because you know three languages, but we are in Hawaii, yeah? We speak our tongue."

"Yes kupunawahine." The table laughs and I continue to eat my food. I love my family.

*****End of Flashback*****

"Hey, you need to be in proper swimwear sir." My eyes open to see a lifeguard hovering over me. I stand up and shake out my hair.

"Sorry about that." He nods and I follow him out of the water.

The two surfers left. The waves have calmed down and a minor piece of my heart has stopped aching. Maybe remembering him isn't such a terrible thing. Maybe I need to remember him because I sure as hell never want to forget him.

***

Arabella

Running up to my room, I ignore the worried faces of my parents and slam my door closed. I curl up in my bed and bawl my eyes out because I don't want to think and I don't want to talk. I just want to cry.

I haven't cried in so long. I've always hated crying because it would remind me of when I was younger and naïve and believed that the mean words people would say to me would eventually stop. I was so young and so stupid that I would run home and cry almost every day, and all of that crying did nothing to stop the pain. So instead I stopped crying. I stopped crying altogether because all it did was make me weaker. But I can't stop it now.

Years and years of pent up anger and hatred towards myself and all who have wronged me pour out of me through these damn tears. I cry and cry until I feel so numb and cold that I can't even open my eyes and then I just stop. Inside I am waiting to hear from any of the voices in my head, anything to tell me something about what to do, but all I hear is silence, and that leaves me unnerved.

Everything that Darien said to me was so true and so harsh that even Lydia seems like a saint. And that's what hurts the most. That he can still love me even though he knows I'm messed up. That he still wants me even though he left me. That he will wait for me… why?

"WHY? WHY? WHY!" A soft knock on the door forces me to open my eyes.

"Come in." I croak out.

I smell mom's perfume and face the door. She and dad stand there with a soft smile on their faces and their arms extended towards me.

"I will not get you to talk to me right now, instead I will sit right beside you and pet your hair like I used to, is that ok?"

I nod my head and scoot over on the bed so mom can do as she said. Resting my head on her lap, I feel the tears build up again and I cry once more. All throughout my pointless tears, my mom hums quietly while petting my hair. I feel dad sit on the edge of the bed and he pats my leg. They soothe, relax and calm me down. They give me the comfort and the love I've been denying myself from for too long. They're the security blanket that I've been too headstrong to fall into. The strength and light to my frail and hollow self.

I don't know how long I'm resting on her lap, but when I re-open my swollen eyes, I notice the sun has gone down. Feeling no more tears, I force myself to talk to them. To talk at all.

"Darien broke up with me." Mom keeps petting my hair slowly.

"I thought you said you two weren't together in that way." I shake my head squeeze her leg.

"We were mom. Oh my God, we were. From the moment he started following me around we became a couple... I was just too scared to acknowledge it."

"Why Arabella?" Dad asks gently. I bury my face further into mom's lap and try to breathe.

"Because I hate myself..." Saying those words out loud feels so painful. To admit such a horrible truth is harder and crueler than anything I've ever done. When neither responds I know they want me to explain, so I try to.

"I guess it started from when I was a child. Kids like Lydia would say the meanest things to me, and I had heard them so much and so often that I guess I believed them. I believed that I was ugly and a freak and that no one would ever like me and I pushed away any and everyone I could because I didn't think I deserved that happiness."

"Oh, Arabella honey that's not good." Sighing heavily I look up into my mother's frowning face.

"I know… well, I know that now. It's–It's something Darien had said to me, about me making up the evil words and nasty stares, about me inflicting harm and pain upon myself mentally even when it was never happening. I didn't even know I was doing it half the time. It just felt so normal to me… so right. Like it was what I meant to feel. It's sick, and it's crazy and it's not normal… I think I need help." Mom nods her head and motions for me to sit up.

"Your father, brothers and I are here for you in any way we can. I know it hasn't been easy on you to have such special eyes but that's what they are Arabella, they're special. They're beautiful and they're you–"

"Because you are you and we are just us and that's all that matters." I say without thinking. Mom looks at me, confused.

"What does that mean?" I shrug and remove my hair from my neck.

"It's something Darien would say to me whenever he would try to explain why he loved me." She nods and leans back against my headboard.

"So what are you going to do about that?" Dad asks. Moving to sit next to me, I lean back with them and rest my head on his shoulder.

"I will do what he told me to do…" I look out the window and see the moon shining and I let go of my last tear.

"I will learn to love myself."

Kupunakane – Grandpa Kupunawahine – Grandma Lau Lau – a specialty dish with pork and salmon Lolo – Crazy/Stupid Ohana – Family Makuahine – Mother Keikikane – Son Keiki - Child

Twenty-Two

Starting Again

Darien

"I think we should go back to Honolulu this summer."

It's been a month since I broke up with Arabella and I've been trying to do anything I can to keep myself away from her. We haven't spoken since that Saturday and it's been so hard to handle. It was one thing not seeing her on the weekend but because I altered my schedule to hers, I have to see her every other day, all the time.

And she always smells so good and looks so beautiful and is so damn perfect! Damn, I want her back so badly I physically ache every time I see or hear her. I never realized I fell so hard for her. Have I said it hurts to see her and not be with her? Because it does.

"Oh Darien, are you sure you want to do that?" Mom asks as we wash the dishes together.

"I'm sure... I need to you know? I can't keep running away from it. From him. I miss Hani so much and completely ignoring everything he was to me is unhealthy. I want to see my kupunakane and kupunawahine; I want to go to the beaches. I want to surf again and I want to... I want to visit his grave and walk where we last stood together... I need to." Tears fall down mom's face and I pull her into me.

"I'm so proud of you, kuʻuipo. Your father and I never wanted to push or rush you to grieve properly we just wanted you to live again and it seems this girl helped you." Again my heart pangs at the thought of Arabella…

Valentine's day is coming up soon and I will spend it alone. Before our breakup I had everything planned out perfectly, it would be romantic and sweet and then we'd kiss and make-out and push our limits… that was what we would do. Now… now I just want to stare at her picture and dream her with me. How pitiful.

"Yeah she… I–I… I can't talk about her yet mom. It still hurts." Mom rubs a soapy hand on my shoulder and smiles sadly.

"I understand. I do." We continue to wash in silence and I have to focus on my breathing so I can stop thinking about Arabella.

"So tell me about this trip, Darien. What do you want to do? Where do you want to go? When do you think we should call your grandparents?" Laughing I hug my mom and kiss her cheek.

"Slow down, makuahine!" We both laugh some more and finish the dishes.

***

Arabella

When I was alone and single I always hated Valentine's Day because it shoved in my face that there are people out there that can be happy and loved and that it would never happen to me. But now that I've met Darien and had a taste of love, I know that this Valentine's Day will be the most painful day ever.

They decorate the halls at school with red and pink hearts and little cupids. Everyone seems to hold hands and making Kissy faces with each other and I am alone… without Darien. I can't believe it took me so damn long to realize how much he meant to me!

"Hey, don't look so pouty I told you, you can spend the V-Day with Taylor and me." I grin at Chelsey and continue our walk to writing class.

"And I told you I'm not interested in being a third wheel, thank you very much. Besides, you guys get very touchy quickly." She rolls her eyes and we walk into class.

Darien is already there, working with Chelsey's partner Austin. We haven't spoken to each other in a month. I thought a few days without him were lonely... I did not understand. It's like I could say something to him, anything at all, but I can't. The words always die in my throat and I end up looking like a gaping fish.

The worst part is, is that he was right. After the whole Dean and cops bullying scare, everyone seemed to move on from me. Especially since Lydia was the one who was instigating it from the very beginning.

No one cared that I have two unique eye colours, if anything people were always saying how cool it was, or how they tried to put in two different colored contacts but it never looked as good as my eyes. At first I thought it was a joke or some kind of prank, but then I thought about what Darien said and realized it was all real. These people who I deemed pure evil were nice, and it was so surprising. I could live a life of peace weeks ago, but I didn't think I was worthy of it.

How sad is that?

"Well, I'm just saying the offer is still open." Shaking my head I sit down and take out my fountain pen and notebook.

"Thank you Chels really, but I will probably spend V-Day with my family." Her nose scrunches up and her head tilts.

"There's nothing romantic about that." I roll my eyes and smirk.

"That's the point." She laughs and hits my arm, something she's been doing a lot.

When I returned to school after the fight with Darien, Chelsey knew something was off with me. Now I wouldn't have called her my friend before because she wasn't but we'd talk from time to time during class. So when she started talking to me outside of class, it confused me.

Chelsey was persistent in figuring out why I was so sad and gloomy and sort of attached herself to me ever since. I don't mind it; she's pleasant company when she isn't smacking lips with Taylor.

It doesn't help when she wants me to join her after class because she sits with Taylor and Taylor sits with Darien. The first time it happened it was too painful to endure again, so I stuck to Vince's class.

Now Chels will visit me there and I appreciate her effort. I guess next to

Darien she's become my first friend. A female friend who doesn't ridicule and hate me. It's taking a lot of change.

"Did you finish that assignment?" I take it out and hand it to her.

"Jeez I thought I was smart in English and yet next to you I'm nothing."

"You're just as good Chels don't say that. I just have extra time to work on things."

Yeah, because now that Darien left the days seem longer and slower than ever before.

That voice in my head... I'm proud to say it's my own. Not Lydia, or SCG, or any other figment of my imagination. It's just plain old me and that too is taking more adjustment too.

The teacher walks in and the class pipes down. And as usual, I spend my time staring at Darien because he looks so good in his V-neck shirt and tan shorts. His hair is messy and reminds me of when we kissed and I kept running my hands through it. His skin is tanned and his eyes are still dazzling... And I miss him so much.

***

Darien

I spent Valentine's Day alone, and it consisted of me playing first-person shooter video games and eating pizza all night. I stopped eating the pizza halfway through the game though because it reminded me of Arabella.

She loves pizza.

I love her...

Instead, I ordered Chinese and ate until I thought I would pass out. I even drank a few beers hoping it would knock me out because oddly enough I could smell her on my clothes.

I always hated doing laundry... but that night I washed everything in sight.

***

Arabella

Valentine's Day wasn't as terrible as I thought it would be because I had my family to cheer me up. We bought pizza, watched movies and played board games.

That day I really appreciated the gift of family and then I remembered that

Darien wouldn't be able to say the same because he didn't have any siblings to fool around with anymore.

I spent the rest of the night crying for the loss of his brother.

***

Darien–Two Months Later

The cursor hovers over the "book" icon and I can taste the hesitation in me. If I book this trip, it means I won't be able to run anymore. I won't be Darien Petros, I'll be Kai Petros again. All the pain and joy in this island will come back to me at full force. Closing my eyes, I envision me and Hani floating in the sea and hear the sharp click of the mouse.

There's no turning back now.

***

Arabella–Two Months Later

"I'm glad you've come here, Arabella." I bite my lip and close the door to the pastor's office.

"Yeah, I just... I've dealt with so many counselors and psychiatrists and they've done nothing for me but tell me to breathe. Something in me knew that I'd find help with you." He smiles and motions to the chair in front of him.

"Have a seat dear and let's talk." Sitting down slowly, I take in my surroundings and take a deep breath. I'm about to address things that are so dark and haunting that I'm scared to even think about it. I'm going to release the pain and aggression and try to get over the hurt I've caused myself. I can finally start again.

There's no turning back now.

ku'uipo - sweetheart

makuahine - mother

kupunakane and kupunawahine – grandpa and grandma

Twenty-Three

Eia Au, Eia 'Oe - Here I am, Here you are

FOUR MONTHS LATER
Darien

"I can't believe you're leaving already mo'opuna!" My grandma pulls me in for another bone-crushing hug.

"Kupunawahine we've been here all summer!" She puts me at arm's length and frowns.

"My mo'opuna leaves Hawaii and never comes back. No call, no mail, nothing. He returns five years later and only spend three months with me? You expect me to want to let you leave?" I sigh and hug her again. She has a point.

"I'm sorry kupunawahine you're right. It was just hard, you know?"

"Mahalo E Ke Akua No Keia La! You have healed your broken heart and grieved with full tears. Aloha Au Ia 'Oe Kai."

"I love you too, kupunawahine." She kisses my forehead five more times before she lets me go. I go to my grandpa to hug him goodbye and he kisses my cheek.

"Kipa hou mai Kai." I nod at his request.

"I will come back as soon as I can and hopefully next time it won't just be me and the family." Grandpa nods and claps me on the back.

"Yes moʻopuna! You better bring this girl here soon, yeah? I want to make sure she is worthy of my boy."

"All right makuahine we need to go before we miss our flight." Mom says hugging and kissing both her parents. Dad is already in the car and we still have one more stop before we go to the airport.

"Aloha ʻoe!" Grandma yells as we drive off.

I stick my head out of the window and wave goodbye as the tiny house gets smaller and smaller. When we stop again and I see where we are I am not afraid.

Getting out of the car, I walk to the beach and take out my surfboard from the trunk. Mom and dad wait in the car as I make the trek to the last place I had seen Hani alive. There's a little shrine made in honor of him and my eyes mist at all the kind words and pictures people placed for him. Scanning the horizon, the memory of that night plays in my mind again and I embrace it.

I will forever miss Hani and I will forever regret that day, but I will remember my brother for what he was and what his name stood for, happiness.

"A hui hou kakou Hani." I place the surfboard next to the shrine and say goodbye to my brother for the first time in five years.

***

Arabella

"Are you sure you don't want to go?" I smile at mom and shake my head no.

"The pastor and I spoke about it and we both realized that I am ready to start again. I don't need my sessions with him anymore. I'm breaking free of the hardships I put on myself." She pulls me in for a hug.

"It's so wonderful to hear that, Arabella. We are so proud of you. Aren't we boys?" My brothers all turn to me and rush to hug me. Being hugged by three massive guys is not in the least bit comfortable, but I embrace it, anyway.

"We are." Adrian says hugging me close.

"Yeah, you're like a whole new person! I mean look at your clothes… you're like showing off your body… ew." Alec says pulling away. I laugh at him and stick out my tongue.

"I'm just happy to see you wearing your hair in different styles. You're a beautiful kid, and if any guy says otherwise–"

"I will handle it." I say to Adam. He smiles and kisses the top of my head. We all leave the church and I send the pastor an enormous smile. He nods in my direction and continues to talk to a family.

"Hey Arabella!" My long braids swivel toward my name and my heart stops at the thought of Darien being here, but I know he isn't.

I don't know where he went when school finished, but he's been away for months without a word. I was angry at first that he would do that to me, but when I told the pastor about it, he said that this may have been something that he needed to do and saying goodbye to me again would only make it harder. I guess he was right.

"Hey!" A hand on my shoulder causes me to jump and I see Benji behind me.

"Oh, hi Benji." He smiles wide.

"I just wanted to see if you were doing anything this Friday? Maybe we could hang out?" He's sweet and sincere but I couldn't if I tried. My heart… my love belongs to Darien, and it feels so good to know that.

"If we were to hang out as friends then I'm ok with that. Anything more I can't do… there's someone that's been waiting a long time for me. I can't let him down." Benji's face falls as I say this.

"Oh, I get it… well, he's a lucky guy. Maybe some other time, then. See you for Friday service." He walks away and I go back to my family. Getting in the car, Alec nudges my side.

"I guess you gave him the grave news?"

"What grave news is that?"

"That you're taken." I blush and look out the window.

"He took it like a trooper." My brothers laugh.

"Yeah, him and every other guy that's asked you out the past few months." Alec responds.

"Yeah that was a disaster! How many was it mom?" Adrian asks.

"I think six?" She responds.

"Seriously! I told you that in confidence!" Mom turns to look at me from the front and smiles.

"Sweetheart there's nothing wrong with letting your brothers know that guys like you. They seem to care!"

"Yeah besides who will sweep up all the broken hearts you've left behind?" Adam says grinning.

Everyone in the car laughs, and I shake my head. They're such weirdos.

***

"Why didn't you go to that formal party thing again? It's not like a zillion guys didn't ask you to go with them." Chelsey asks as she licks the dripping ice cream from her hand.

We're spending the day at the mall because she wanted to do a little back to school shopping. She mainly bought clothes, and I bought two dresses. I wore one of them now. It makes me feel pretty.

"I've never liked those kinds of events. Too flashy for me. Besides…" *I wanted to go with Darien, but he never asked me.*

"Right so what are you going to do this year?" I smile in gratitude for the subject change.

"Well, since I'm going to graduate, I don't feel the pressure of continuing my education so soon. I need the time to think and find myself… as cliché as that sounds." She nods her head and glances to my left. I watch her squint at whatever the object is before she shakes her head and looks me up and down.

"Man Arabella that dress looks amazing on you. Seriously, your boobs look great! And who knew you had such a nice booty!" I slap her arm to shut her up because she's speaking way too loudly. This girl can never stay focused on one topic.

"Come on, you said it's not that revealing!" She shakes her head and keeps smiling.

"It isn't. It just suits you very well." I glance down at the dress and smile softly. The dress is plain; it's two tones of peach with spaghetti straps and a crisscross back. The middle is cinched, so the waist looks slimmer and it falls at my knees. I like it because it's loose and light and doesn't show off too much skin.

"Thank Chels."

"You're welcome. You should wear dresses more often." She says pulling at my strap.

"Ok, ok let's move on. What are you doing this year?"

"Well, I'm dropping graphic design and going to Anaheim U for an MFA in Digital Filmmaking."

"WOW! That sounds amazing!"

"Yup!" She's got such an excited buzz around her; I can't wait till I experience that.

"What is Taylor doing?" Her eyes land on something on my left again before she responds.

"He wants to get a Masters in entrepreneurship. Who would have guessed?" We both laugh and her eyes widen before they shift down to the table in front of her.

"What's wrong Chels–"

"Arabella." My body freezes.

My name has never sounded so good before and I feel like I haven't heard that voice in years. I get out of my seat and turn to see a very tan looking Darien.

"Darien." My voice is much quieter than I want it to be. I watch his eyes graze over every inch of my body, taking in the sight of me. They linger on my breasts, my lips, my legs, my stomach and then on my face.

"You're wearing a dress." He comments. I blush and his gaze travels over my skin.

"Yeah."

"And your hair has changed." I nod, making my braids shake. His eyes watch that movement too.

"You look so sexy." I blush even harder and begin to squirm under his penetrating gaze. He licks his lips and steps closer to me.

"Thank you."

"I'm just going to keep shopping. Text me Ari!" I hear Chelsey's voice somewhere in the background, but it's like all sounds drown out except

Darien's.

"Will you come with me?" His hand reaches out and I take it slowly.

He grabs my bags and leads me out of the mall and straight to his car. We drive in silence to this unknown destination, all the while my heart is pounding like a jackhammer. I'm sweating so much and my legs won't stop shaking. I've been dreaming about this day for so long, but I can barely get the words out to say something. I wring my hands in my lap and try to relax, but I'm failing miserably.

The car pulls to a stop and I notice we are at that park again. The park where he told me about his brother... and then ended our relationship. Darien comes around to open my door for me and we walk. I'm struggling to walk normally while Darien looks so composed.

"Arabella?" We've stopped at the bridge and I have to hold on to something to keep me standing.

"Yes Darien?" We both lock eyes and I can see his eyes blazing with an emotion I can't seem to name.

"How are you?" His question surprises me.

I open my mouth to say something, but it shuts closed. I try again, but I fail. Instead, I walk up to him tripping twice on nothing and touch his face. My hands are shaking, but I trace the face I've missed so much. His eyes close at my touch and I smile at the thought he may still love me.

Going on the tips of my toes, I press my lips to his chin since I can't reach his mouth. I continue to kiss any part I can until he leans down and kisses me. A jolt of electricity goes through us and we pull back to look at each other. I love this boy. So damn much.

Darien grabs me into him and growls low. His lips are hard and wet and he's making my head spin. He kisses me with full possession and every part of me is on fire for him. Trailing down from my lips to my neck, and my breasts, he licks and sucks on my skin and even bites areas. We're on each other like animals; hands roaming, breaths panting, eyes rolling, areas hardening. When we finally slow down, I force out the words that mean so much to me.

"Darien... I–I love you." He pulls back slowly and kisses my forehead.

"Ho'i Hou Ke Aloha teleiótita." I don't know what he said but it sounds

Hawaiian. Maybe that's where he went this summer.

"What does that mean?" Kissing me tenderly and passionately, he nibbles on my lip before he responds.

"Let's fall in love all over again, teleiótita." I melt into a puddle at his feet and kiss him again. This is what I deserve. This is what I've been waiting for.

Darien.

The boy who's changed everything.

To Be Continued...

Moʻopuna - Grandchild
  Kupunawahine - Grandma
  Mahalo E Ke Akua No Keia La–Thanks be to God for this day
  Aloha Au Ia ʻOe–I love you
  Kipa hou mai—Come visit again
  Makuahine - Mother
  Aloha ʻoe – Farewell to you
  A hui hou kakou – Until we meet again

About the Author

Myah Catherine is a young and happily married mother of one, who loves to read and write just as much as she loves Netflix and Disney Plus. She aspires to create stories that connect with all generations and go against the norm. Writing Christian Fiction, Young Adult and Romance helps her reflect on her own view of relationships and faith, and on her love for Christ, while at the same time connecting with today's youth on issues like maturity, love, and their struggles with their own beliefs. When she's not reading, writing, or binge-watching TV shows, you can find her on any of her various game systems.

Also by Myah Catherine

ROOM 1815

Twenty-something year old Talon is running for his life. With only his dad and his wits to guide him, he's been keeping his pursuers at bay for almost four years ... but living a life on the run isn't a life worth living.

Talon's life changes the day he enters Room 1815. Brought face-to-face with mortality, love, and the claims of Jesus Christ, he must make critical decisions about his future, both temporal and eternal. Filled with suspense, action, and a gripping love story, Room 1815 will captivate readers and keep them hanging on to the final, shocking, page!

Manufactured by Amazon.ca
Bolton, ON